Fiction   JUL 0 9 2004

Mitcheltree, Tom
Blink of an eye

$ 24.95
2003-21177

BLINK OF AN EYE

Other Novels
by Tom Mitcheltree

Dataman
Katie's Will
Katie's Gold
Merry Little Christmas
Terror in Room 201

BLINK OF AN EYE

by
Tom Mitcheltree

INTRIGUE PRESS | DENVER

Copyright ©2004 Tom Mitcheltree
Published by:
Intrigue Press, PO Box 102004, Denver, CO 80210
An imprint of Corvus Publishing

All rights reserved. No part of this book may be reproduced or
transmitted in any form or by any means, electronic or mechanical,
including photocopying, recording, or by an information storage and
retrieval system—except by a reviewer who may quote brief passages
in a review—without permission in writing from the publisher.

Printed and bound in the United States of America

This book is a work of fiction. Names, characters, places and
incidents are either the product of the author's imagination or
are used fictitiously. Any resemblance to actual events or locales
or persons, living or dead, is entirely coincidental. Although
the author and publisher have made every effort to ensure the
accuracy and completeness of information contained in this book,
we assume no responsibility for errors, inaccuracies, omissions,
or any inconsistency herein. Any slights of people, places or
organizations are unintentional.

Book layout and design by Magpie Creative Design

Library of Congress Cataloging-in-Publication Data

Mitcheltree, Tom, 1946-
  Blink of an eye / by Tom Mitcheltree.
    p. cm.
  ISBN 1-890768-53-7
  I. Title.
  PS3613.I87B56 2004
  813'.6--dc22

                                          2003021177

10 9 8 7 6 5 4 3 2 1

To Paris, a city that inspires.

ONE

He pulled open the tall French windows and leaned in the frame, one hand resting on the wrought-iron railing that kept him from tumbling from the room to the narrow street four floors below. He stared across the street, more of an alley, wide enough for just one lane, to the granite façade of the building across the way. The granite was light tan, cut into large blocks and offset only by the narrower blocks that bordered the high, arched windows directly across from him. The building was butted between two others, each of a similar color but of a different design. The windows on one were rectangular and shuttered. The windows on the other were tall and narrow, too, but cased in wood painted white.

He could see into the rooms across the way. The first was an office with three desks in it. The second had a conference table in its center, piled high with papers and books.

This was Paris in June. The temperature usually topped out around seventy-five to eighty degrees during the day. The sun felt good, so he stayed in the open window and stared at the office on the other side of the narrow street, watching the granite on the side of the building take on different shades of tan as the sun moved across the sky. Occasionally clouds would block the sunshine, and then the building would change its colors again.

He had come a long way to be in this window. The idea of actually living and working in Paris was simply indescribable—people dream of such an opportunity. He may well have made a mistake taking on a change so great as this was to his life, but he needed something to happen. He found little satisfaction in the life he was living before, but he'd been complacent about it, feet stuck in mud. He'd been watching the mud dry. One day a man with whom he had worked had shown him a flyer about a job in Paris. The job itself did not seem very interesting to him, but Paris did. Four months later he was leaning in an open window, staring at an office to which he would report the next day.

He did not think in terms of mistakes. He thought in terms of choices made that had not led to the desired results. When that happened, he made new choices. But for that one time, he never looked back. In the darkness of an alley, in the heat of a summer night, in a part of a city rich with poverty, he had made a choice and shot a fourteen-year-old black boy to death. The boy had a knife. In the sliver of light that penetrated the alley the glint from the blade made it look as much a gun as anything. In the blink of an eye he had made a choice.

The boy was dead before he hit the ground. If he had known it was a knife, he would have handled it a different way. He was cleared. The boy was trouble. The rioting that took place after the white cop shot the black boy was only half-hearted and modestly destructive. Even his neighborhood knew the boy was trouble, destined to the kind of death that took him.

That was the only time he'd shot someone, and, unlike everything else that had come before, he had not been able to put it behind him. The shout to stop, the whirling around of the boy in the darkness of the alley, the flash of light from the steel of the blade, the three shots neatly centered in the boy's chest, and then the realization, finally, of what he had done: followed by two hundred nights, two hundred nightmares.

Paris hovered in the distance like Nirvana each time he woke to the sounds of his own moans, his sweat soaking another set of sheets.

TWO

The young couple staggered from the jazz club, Caveau de la Huchette, as much intoxicated by the 1920s music they had just listened to as by the copious amounts of champagne and wine they'd consumed between dances. Near two in the morning, the couple, both in their early twenties, was now running on youthful reserves of energy. They laughed giddily as they leaned into each other for balance, and together they let the cool night air sweep some of the heat from their bodies.

Although she'd only met him that evening, she'd decided to let him come back to her room. As exhausted as she was by an evening that stretched from the dangerous, thus truly appealing, nightclubs of Pigalle to the Caveau on the left bank of the Seine, she was still up to ending the night in the arms of a strong, tall, handsome, Latin lover, who's love for pushing limits echoed hers.

For his part, he couldn't believe his luck. During his first night in Paris to visit his parents he found himself with a beautiful, blonde American girl with the body of a goddess and the face of an angel. His parents would be furious when they didn't find him in his bed in the morning, but for this he was willing to risk their wrath.

She needed a moment to get her bearings, and then she smiled at her stupidity. La Rue du Chat-Qui-Pêche, the narrowest street in Paris, was just a few doors down la Rue de la Huchettè, and it led back to le Petit Pont. The bridge would take them to the island where Notre Dame is situated, and eventually to her hotel, the Hôtel de Crillon.

As she turned the corner into the alley, dragging her soon-to-be lover with her, she wondered what kind of a reaction she might get back at the hotel. Would the concierge or the desk clerk dare raise an eyebrow at the sight of her lover du jour? Doubtful. They are paid to indulge and service the rich. And if they didn't, she would see to it that they would get fired.

La Rue du Chat-Qui-Pêche was no more than an alley, and the two of them brushed shoulders as they made their way down it. The alley itself was dark at this time of night, but where it opened up to the next block the bright lights along the Seine illuminated their way.

A slight noise behind them caused the girl to glance back. In the light of the street behind them she saw the silhouette of a man. Although she couldn't see his features, she recognized him from the shape of his body as someone who had been in the Caveau. Just for a moment she thought it odd that she could recognize his silhouette because that was all that she had seen in the club, too. He had stood back against the wall in the shadows. His face had been no more than shades of gray and black. On another night, if she had been alone, she might have drifted back to the shadows to see if his face was more interesting than his body had been. Leaning casually against a wall, his body had blended into the shadows, which didn't completely hide the fact that he was a bit overweight. Overweight could be interesting, she thought. She smiled to herself. Such thoughts. She'd had too much to drink.

She curled her arm tightly inside of Escobar's and hurried him a little. She was anxious to get him in her bed.

The man behind them smiled, too. He had made sure

that she had noticed him in the club. He counted on her seeing him and then dismissing him. Late at night in a dark alley it amazed him how little it took for someone to throw caution to the wind. He quickened his pace so that he closed on the couple ahead of him, but he did not move so fast they could sense him coming. When he was within ten feet of the two, he glanced back to make sure no one was behind him and then over the shoulders of the two to make sure no one was coming the other way. An alley this narrow in such a popular part of Paris was not an ideal spot, but it was the only opportunity the two had given him.

She was the first to sense it, as he thought she would, women being more cautious than men in the dark of night, but by the time she started to turn her head it was already too late. The sound was little more than a puff of air. Suddenly the beautiful girl next to Escobar was dead weight pulling him down with her. The expression on Escobar's face was midway between laughter and surprise, and his body had just started to turn toward the girl when the second puff dropped him in a heap on top of the girl.

Each had been shot at the base of the skull with a hollow-point .22 bullet. Neither was dead yet. The bullets had done considerable damage, but the lead had mushroomed and plowed just below the surface of the brain. If the man had walked away at that point, both the young man and young woman would more than likely have survived the assault on their lives, but neither would have been vibrant again.

The man had no intention of letting them live. One he had been sent to kill. The other could be a witness. He put the muzzle of the silencer first in the little recess just in front of the girl's left ear and fired again. Next he turned the girl's head with the toe of his shoe and leaned down to put the silencer and the barrel of the gun into her mouth, shoving it in deep until he hit the soft tissue at the back of her throat before he fired again. He repeated this with the young man.

By the time he stepped over their bodies to walk down the alley toward the Seine, they were both dead. Walking across the bridge at Petite Pont, he casually slipped the gun from his coat pocket and dropped it over the railing. It made only a slight sound when it hit the water.

He was just another carefree tourist, walking back to a hotel in Paris late at night on a June evening; at least that's all that anyone would remember if he had been seen on the street. He was anything but carefree. His mind clicked over the business of murder to make sure that he had not overlooked something. The alley was still wet with rain. It was also a favorite spot for the late night partying crowd who got caught up short. Far too many drunks urinated in alleys and on the steps leading down to the Seine, he thought. In the morning, the smell of urine was overpowering. In this case, though, it was a blessing. The rain and the urine would make crime-scene forensics a nightmare.

Even in the Caveau, he had been cautious. He had extended his arm between two people at the bar and his face had been behind the head of one of them when he ordered a beer. He had turned his head away when he paid the cover charge at the door. No one had seen his face straight on. He had remained in the shadows, away from other people.

And even if they were to drag the river and find the gun, what would they find? A homemade silencer, untraceable. A gun with no serial numbers. Common ammunition. No fingerprints. But they wouldn't find the gun. Paris police were not that enthusiastic, even when it came to solving murders.

He laughed to himself as he crossed the bridge and walked in front of the large building on the other side. He had killed the couple within two blocks of the Prefecture de Police.

THREE

For a moment the three sized each other up without saying a word. The woman sat at one desk and the man sat casually on the corner of another. He looked from one to the other, and then he let his gaze drift out the window to the wrought-iron balcony and French windows across the way. With the curtains open he could look into his room and see the small desk, the armchair, the armoire, and in the shadows of the room, the double bed. From here he could just glimpse into what had once been a closet and was now a bathroom with a sink and a shower crammed into it. The toilet was across the hall from his room.

He glanced back at the man and woman. Dale Bailey was in his mid-forties, his hair gray at the temples and thin on top, his body far from athletically trim, and his complexion very pale, as if he hadn't seen much sun in a long, long time. He was dressed in a tailored, dark blue pinstripe suit, and he wore black shoes that were shined to a brilliance. The woman, Jill St. Claire, was dressed in a conservative black skirt with matching jacket, and a white blouse. For a little flare she had a silk scarf tied at her neck, the soft pink ends hanging down between her breasts. She had breasts, he noted, that even the suit jacket could not conceal. He suspected she had nice legs buried beneath the desk as well. Like Dale, she was pale, but on her it looked better. Her hair was auburn and her eyes were green. She wasn't cute or pretty but handsome in the way a mature woman can be handsome, although he guessed that she wasn't much over thirty. He thought she might have been plain in her youth, and that she was now growing into attractiveness as she matured.

Dale was surprised by Grant Reynolds' appearance. He had read the man's file and he had seen the black-and-white photos, but neither had prepared him for the man. Grant had broad shoulders and narrow hips, and he looked taller than the six-two listed in the file. The pictures made him look heavy. Grant didn't look heavy in person. He had the leanness of a basketball player, but one with muscles. And he didn't look sinister in person. The black-and-white photos brought out shadows that were not there on the real man.

Jill felt her pulse quicken just a bit as she looked at the new man. He was ... well, he was damned handsome. He had dark, thick, black hair cut moderately short, with just a hint of gray flecked along the temples. For a man who was only thirty-six, this gave him a look of maturity that stretched well beyond those years. His eyes were gray/blue, and they held hers in a steady gaze when she spoke to him. His face was a little weathered, not so much by the sun, but maybe by wind and cold. She knew from his file that he liked to sail and to hike.

He was nicely dressed, but the dark gray suit he wore looked to her like it was off the rack. He might be one of those fortunate few who looked good in anything he put on. He did not look like a man who would bother to have a suit tailored for him. The only thing she did not like about him from first impressions, and she was a woman who believed in first impressions, was the hint of a five-o'clock shadow. Obviously he had shaved recently, yet already his beard was pushing its way back to the surface. He might well be a man who had to shave twice a day.

Dale motioned him to the third desk in the room. "That will be yours," he said. He nodded toward the door that led into the next room. "That's our workroom," he said.

Grant glanced at the door and then back to Dale. "Do you mind if I sit down?" he asked.

Jill smiled to herself. Grant was being politically correct for the moment, but he wasn't one to ask for permission to do much of anything, if she had read his file right. He was his own man, and Dale, technically his boss, wouldn't be able to control Grant any more than he could control her.

"Please do," Dale said. While Grant tried out the chair behind the empty desk, Dale opened a file on his desk. "I'd like to go over a few things with you," he said.

Grant nodded his head once, and then bent over in the chair to find the knobs underneath it to adjust it to his size. Other than clothes, few things were built to his size. He was used to making adjustments.

"Let me make sure this background information is correct," Dale said. "You have a B.A. in literature, is that right?" He exaggerated a quizzical expression to make sure that he found a degree in literature to be odd to say the least.

"It was a Bachelor of Fine Arts, and yes, the major was in literature," Grant said. For some reason, the people in the line of work he'd chosen, no matter where they had been, had found a degree in literature an oddity.

"Then you served in the army for four years and came out of it a captain. That's pretty fast for the army, second lieutenant to captain in four years."

Grant shrugged. The army had rhyme and reason to it that even he, the man who liked to analyze literature, could not fathom. "I was in Military Intelligence and did good work. The army noticed and tried to keep me by promoting me quickly."

"But they didn't keep you."

"I got out and became a cop."

"Four years. You went from rookie to sergeant."

Jill injected here, "And then you quit, joined a force in a much larger city, and became a homicide detective."

He looked from one to the other, wondering just what it was that was so fascinating about this for the two of them. It was in the file. They could read. His was a life that held few if any secrets. "It's all in the file," he said.

"In the file," Jill added, "it says you were a good detective for six years, that you earned pay raises and promotions quickly, and that, in the middle of all of this, you chose to work nights so you could get a law degree."

"You even passed the bar," Dale volunteered.

"The two tend to go hand in hand," Grant said. "The law degree and the bar."

"But you never practiced law," Jill said. "Instead, once you got your license, you quit your job to take this one."

Grant slid back in his chair to the wall behind him, put his hands behind his head, and lifted his feet onto the desktop. He nearly smiled when the other two shared a horrified look between them. People in this type of job didn't put feet on desktops. He didn't care what they thought. He wanted them on the defensive because he knew where they would go next with the file.

"Did your change of plans have anything to do with shooting the boy?"

"Everyone tells me it was a clean shoot," he said.

"Do you have some doubt in your mind about that?" Jill asked.

Every night, he wanted to say, but instead he turned his steady gaze to her and said, "'Clean shoot' is a contradiction of terms. There's nothing clean about it. Not the mess you make of the kid, not the mess you generate in paperwork, and not the mess you make of your emotional life.

I was in a dark alley with a dangerous kid who was armed—
I had to decide whether or not to shoot. It's not a decision
you get to reconsider once it's made."

"You won't be carrying a gun in this job," she said.

His gaze remained unwavering. "That was one of its
appeals."

"Ever." Dale added. "If you are involved in any incident
with a gun, we cannot, will not, protect you from the police.
It is a given with them that you will not carry a gun."

"They don't want me to have a gun, you don't want me
to have a gun, and I don't want me to have a gun. Can we
move on?"

Jill could not keep herself from smiling. She had read
his file carefully. He had size, he had quickness, and he had
training in the martial arts. He could do plenty of damage
without a gun. She changed the subject. "You've never
married," she said.

"So?" he asked.

"I just found that odd. I don't run across too many attractive men your age who have never married," she said.

"You mean men who are straight."

"I wasn't suggesting you were gay—"

"If I were, the FBI would have figured that out when
they did the rather extensive background check on me,
and then they wouldn't have offered me this job. Are you
married, Dale?"

"Divorced," he said. "The job ..." He let the words trail off.

"And you, Jill?"

"The career comes first," she said.

"Lesbian?"

"Not to my knowledge," she said, smiling. *Touché,* she
thought.

"Now that we have established that we're antisocial lon-
ers, can we move on to the job?"

Again the two of them glanced at each other. They had been nervous about Grant before they ever met him. He was good, he moved up the ranks quickly, yet he never stayed put very long. He was rootless. When he left a place, he left it for good. He made friends, but he didn't keep them once he moved on. He was a Teflon man who didn't let things stick to him. The shooting, though, said something else about him. Apparently some things he could not leave behind. How dangerous did that make him?

Dale leaned forward, folded his hands in his lap, and stared at them as he spoke. This was a ploy with him. He wanted to impress Grant with his knowledge about the job. He wanted to do it without notes or manuals. He wanted to make it clear that he was the expert here.

"First of all, let me make it clear that you are not an FBI agent, you are not an employee of the FBI, nor are you to be considered, even remotely, an associate of the FBI."

"But the FBI recommended that I be hired for the job."

That forced Dale to look up from his hands. That steady gaze was directed at him. The lips had on them just a hint of smile. "I won't bullshit you. You are a field representative for the FBI, but that is not how you will ever present yourself. You are a bureaucrat first, a GS second, a member of the foreign service third. Officially, you work for the Legat Office in the American Embassy—that's the Legal Attaché's office, which is manned by the FBI. But you are a civil servant working for the foreign service in the embassy."

Jill interrupted Dale, and he wasn't happy about it. She said, "The French police notify us of a major crime involving an American citizen. We do a preliminary investigation, and then we recommend action be taken."

Dale jumped back in. "If it is established that it is a crime by a French national against an American, we leave it with the French police or they never inform us about it in the first place. If it is a crime against an American by any other foreign national, we forward the information either to the FBI or Interpol. The FBI takes it if the crime appears a threat to national security. Interpol and the FBI work together if no threat is perceived. But you don't need to worry about any of that."

Jill explained. "You're a field rep. You do the preliminary investigation and then you turn it over to Dale. He determines where it goes. I'm the one who speaks French fluently. That makes me often a combination field rep and secretary."

"We also do a little public relations for the embassy. Wealthy Americans who get ripped off in Paris tend to get angry and pound on the door of the embassy to demand action. They refer them to us, their 'investigative unit,' to assure the good citizens that their welfare is being looked after."

"From your tone of voice, I get it that you disapprove," Grant said.

Dale said, "You will learn quickly that the police barely tolerate us only as a diplomatic courtesy, that the FBI treats us like grunts who shovel shit for them, and that the foreign service and the diplomatic corps have to be reminded continually of who we are and what we do. If you are looking for us on the totem pole, we're the part stuck in the mud."

"We'll have to see what we can do to get them to remember our names," Grant said, earning another exchange of looks between the other two. "How does Interpol see us?"

"They like us," Jill said. "They see us as an information source that can add to their database."

"Their headquarters is in France, isn't it?" Grant asked.

"In Lyons," Dale said. "Any other questions?"

"Not that I can think of."

"We get paid once a month," Jill said. "You have to pick up your check at the embassy. You get about seven thousand Euro a month for a housing allotment, and another three thousand Euro for meals and transportation. Between the two of them you can get a small apartment on the edge of the city and a lot of time on a metro train. Most of the crime against Americans takes place in the heart of the city, though, because that's the part the tourists love the most."

"We can check out a car from the embassy motor pool, but pulling your own teeth is easier and more fun," Dale said.

The phone on his desk rang. He picked it up and listened for several minutes without saying a word. When he hung up, without saying goodbye, he said, "Shit."

"That doesn't sound good," Jill said.

"They found the bodies of a couple early this morning in la Rue du Chat-Qui-Pêche. Murdered. She turns out to be the granddaughter of an American billionaire and he's the son of a Bolivian diplomat."

"And to whom do we direct this one?" Grant asked.

Dale slowly rose to his feet. "To all of them," he said. "The billionaire is a golfing buddy of the President of the United States. The bodies are still in the alley. The embassy wants us to walk down and take a look."

FOUR

Jill and Grant followed Dale down the four flights of stairs to the street. Over his shoulder he said, "I think the easiest way is just to walk down to le quai St-Michel and then down to the alley."

They followed behind, neither in a hurry to look at dead bodies. "What do you think of Paris?" she asked.

"It's old and low to the ground," Grant remarked, carefully hiding his already growing affection for the city.

She laughed, feeling he was overplaying his aloofness. "Yes, and both are part of its charm, something this city never seems to be short on. The center of the old city was kept low to the ground for a purpose. First, because the city is so old that in its inception tall buildings were beyond anyone's knowledge to build, and second because later planners decided to keep the core of the city like this. Trees, broad boulevards, and lots of parks are the words I would have used to describe Paris in simple and generic terms, but I find it hard to truly define a city so intoxicating with life and culture. You'll start to understand what I mean, in time."

"That's not to say I don't like it," he said, a bit embarrassed with his previous comment. Underneath his cool exterior, he was overwhelmed with the beauty of the bustling Parisians, the niche storefronts, and the palpable distinction between American and European life. He wanted to explore every inch of the city, to taste the delicious scents in the air, to sit in a park and observe Parisians' quirks and attitudes. This was indeed a culture shock for him, although he felt fairly comfortable with how he could assimilate into Paris' tempo.

"Living here and visiting are two different things. If I could live in this section of Paris, I'd like the city a lot more. To live on the outskirts, though, is like living in a residential district of any city in the world. It certainly is less Paris, maybe even less France. Where are you staying?"

"In the hotel across from the office."

"That will do until you find a place."

"I don't plan to find a place. I've made arrangements to stay at the hotel."

"You have to be kidding," she said, twisting her head to see his face. "That will cost you a fortune."

"Not really. I negotiated to pay eight hundred a month, less than the owner would get in the tourist season, but far more than he would get in the off season. He will actually make more on the room this way."

"What will you do for food?"

"Breakfast is included. The owner has agreed to let me use the kitchen in the cellar where the dining room is and to use the refrigerator. Besides, I have a city full of culinary delights at my disposal. I won't be going hungry.

"My room is small, but I travel light. It has a shower and a sink, but the toilet is across the hall. On the other hand, the other four rooms on the same floor all have complete bathrooms, so I'm the only one who uses the communal toilet."

"You are serious," she said.

Of course he was. The things that impressed other people like houses and cars and material goods didn't impress him. He liked to read. He liked to listen to music. He liked to go to movies. He liked to eat in interesting restaurants. None of this cost a lot of money, and from what he could already see and breathe in, Paris catered to each and every one of his personal desires. Besides, he always had more money than he needed. In Paris he could survive on the living allowance they offered, and he could send his paycheck to an investment program he had, one that had already accumulated more money than he could imagine spending.

"Why not?" he asked. "Across the river is a supermarket in the basement of one of the stores. The Metro stop is near the office. If I need to use a phone or a computer, I can find both in the office. Tell me what I'm missing here."

"Space, maybe," she said. "Privacy, a chance to get away from your work, friends ..." She threw up her hands. "Everything!" she said.

"You're talking about yourself, not me. I think I'll do just fine," he said with a secret smile on his face. This city was drawing him in with every street corner, shop, and aged building.

A knot of police gathered at the end of la Rue du Chat-Qui-Pêche where it came out on le quai St-Michel. Paul was already talking to them when Grant and Jill joined him. Smoothly, in what seemed like flawless French to Grant, Jill took over the conversation.

One of the officers separated from the group of policemen and walked into the alley. Within a few minutes he returned, following behind a man who could only be, Grant knew, a homicide detective. Grant knew one when he saw one. For nearly six years he had awakened each morning and in his mirror looked into the eyes of a homicide detective. This man's eyes had that same wide-eyed look with that same shadow of deep despair.

"Inspector Gerard," Dale said, extending a hand to the Frenchman, "I appreciate that you have notified us."

Gerard nodded. "Yes. We are still processing the scene," he said, "and we are waiting for crime scene technicians from Interpol before we remove the bodies. You may walk down the alley to the second window on the right, but I want you to go no farther than that."

Gerard was not as tall as Grant, but he was a large man, Grant noticed, close to six-one and 220 pounds, a bit thick and soft around the waistline. He had a nose a little too long, with heavy black eyebrows, and dark, dark brown eyes. The look in his eyes, Grant thought, and the firm lines of his mouth would not draw women to him, not unless they were looking for someone who might be a little dangerous.

What Grant liked best about the man from the moment he opened his mouth was that his English was very good, nearly without an accent, and Dale spoke to him in a normal voice, not as if he was talking to someone who might not understand him. Grant placed Gerard in his mental log as his first important contact person in Paris.

Grant stood very still and concentrated on what he saw. He believed fully in instinct and intuition. What he saw first and what he felt about it were important to him when it came to crime scenes. To no one but himself, he said, "It was probably very dark in the middle of the alley. Only a few windows and no doorways in the alley. The windows are frosted glass, layered with dirt, or covered from the inside. It is unlikely that anyone would have witnessed the killings, at least not from the windows. Anyone on either end of the alley might have seen the silhouettes of the victims and the killer in the light from the opposite end of the alley, but it is unlikely that a witness would have understood what he or she was seeing."

When he finally refocused his attention back to the group around him, he was surprised to find Dale, Jill, and the inspector staring at him. "I'm sorry," he said. "Did I say that out loud?"

"*Oui*," Gerard said. "You are?"

"I'm sorry," Dale said. "This is Grant Reynolds. He's our newest field representative."

Jill added, "He has four years in military intelligence, four in police work, and six as a homicide detective in Boston. A homicide detective who also earned a law degree from Harvard."

"Agent, *non?*" Gerard asked.

"A field representative," Dale said firmly.

"I see." Gerard made a thoughtful frown, "Come with me and tell me what else you see."

When they reached the second window, Gerard signaled for Dale and Jill to stop, but he motioned Grant to follow him to the bodies. His two co-workers were left to share a surprised look, but Grant was too busy to notice. He was making sure that he followed in the steps of the detective. The crime scene would have been turned into a grid, and the first thing carefully examined would have been a path to the victims. Once the forensics team was done with this, it would become the route back and forth to the bodies until the rest of the grid was examined.

Gerard stopped five feet from the bodies. Grant concentrated on what he saw, and again spoke out loud without realizing he was doing it. "Tapped from behind. Both bodies falling forward, the girl first and then the boy. Neither saw it coming. The girl's arm is still locked in the boy's, and, by the look of their positions, his body folded over hers, and she dragged him down before he got hit.

"Little blood. Small caliber pistol, probably a .22, probably silenced or the echo of shots certainly would have attracted someone. One to the back of the head and one to the temple." He squatted down so he could get a clear view of the girl's mouth, which was still open and had a small trickle of blood that had worked its way through her lips and pooled on her left arm, which was curled under her head.

"Inspector," Grant said. "This was a professional hit. You'll find that each of the victims has a third wound to the head, administered through the soft palate in the mouth. This is a signature tap. You'll find that the killer has a file with Interpol. He's known as 'the Assassin,' and he has perhaps thirty or more hits attributed to him."

Grant rose back to his feet to find the inspector with just a hint of surprise and annoyance on his face. "And you know this as truth?"

"He executed a congresswoman who lived in Boston. She was leading a crusade against corruption in the building industry. She was executed in the aisle of a grocery store—alone in that aisle for no more than ten seconds when she was shot to death, a bullet to the back of the head, one to the temple, and a third to the soft palate. Half a dozen people saw the man, but none could agree on his description. He wore a hat low over his brow. He wore sunglasses and a bulky, long coat. He stooped, or he stood tall on the balls of his feet. People only saw the side of his face, and they never saw him head on. He was medium height to tall and thin to heavy set, with light to dark skin. He killed a woman in the middle of the day in the middle of a crowded grocery store, was seen by a half a dozen people, but was never captured, never identified, and never tied to one piece of forensic evidence. I hear he gets a million dollars a hit, and he's worth every penny."

Gerard slowly nodded his head. "You may be of use to me, Mr. Reynolds. Especially if Interpol confirms what you say."

Grant turned and retraced his steps. Over his shoulder, he said, "Interpol will."

When he reached Dale and Jill, Dale asked, "Interpol will what?"

Grant walked past them, heading back to le quai St-Michel. "Confirm that this was a tap by a hit man called 'the Assassin.'"

Dale was trailing behind him now. "You're telling me this was a professional hit? How can you be so sure?"

"I've seen his handiwork before," Grant said. "I only have one question left."

"Which is?" Jill asked.

"Public taps like these are meant to be a message to someone. Was the message for an American billionaire or for a Bolivian diplomat?"

By the time he reached the end of la Rue du Chat-Qui-Pêche, three people had stopped in their tracks to watch him walk away.

FIVE

He leaned against the sill of the open French windows and sipped his coffee. The air outside was cool, the sun yet to cut through the shadows that filled the narrow street. He thought about his few days in Paris. The essentials had been taken care of. He had a place to stay, his coffeemaker was working—one of the few electronic luxuries he allowed himself beyond the portable CD player with the good set of headphones—, and he had started his new job with a bang.

With a bang. Pop, pop, pop … pop, pop, pop. Hardly a bang, but not noiseless either. No ejected shells at the crime scene. A tidy killer? It was quick and in the dark. Like in the grocery store, the Assassin would not have taken the time to pick up shell casings. He wouldn't have had the time and still feel safe. That meant a revolver, and a revolver could not be silenced completely. A loud puff of air six times over, but not so loud that it would have been noticed beyond the length of the alley.

Planned? That was what made the man so hard to catch. Everything the police knew about him suggested he was a creature of opportunity. He simply followed his victim until the right opportunity came along to kill him or her. A man didn't get away with over thirty impromptu murders unless he had something going for him. Even that defied luck. Grant believed he was an incredibly intelligent man, one who could, like a great chess player, see a dozen moves ahead. When he walked in the alley, following the couple, he would have known that no one was going to come up on him from behind. He couldn't have been sure about the other end of the alley, the one that opened up to the Seine, but he somehow knew he could make the hit and get out the way he came in if he had to.

That meant he was either sure that no one else was around, or he had calculated the movements of anyone else who might have been in the area. Grant went with the second guess. The man was simply brilliant at calculating a window of opportunity. Time and time again he had killed in public and not once been seen doing it.

Grant wondered if the man had calculated the odds of a Boston cop showing up just after his latest hit, a cop who had investigated a previous tap thousands of miles away. Maybe he had the same philosophy about odds that Grant had. Things happened around us more often than we knew, but we were oblivious to them. Odds for almost anything weren't as high as we thought they were.

He closed the French windows and went into the bathroom to rinse his cup in the sink and set it on top of the medicine cabinet. He had already cleaned the little coffeemaker, one that would make only one cup, and put it away. The owner had made it clear that he was to use no appliances in his room. "Fire, *oui,*" he had said.

He slipped on a jacket and left the room. In a few days he had already started a list of contradictions he had found in Paris. Codes against appliances in the room would be strictly enforced, he was told. On the other hand, the access to the dining room was a tightly wound, very steep spiral staircase located in the tiny lobby of the hotel. No handicapped person could have maneuvered down it, and even a child would have had a struggle. No one seemed to object to it.

He had as part of his rent the breakfast of the day, the breakfast of every day: croissants and la confiture, warm, room temperature milk, and a tall pot of thick coffee. It wasn't bad, per say, but it was definitely going to take some getting used to. Especially that bitter chicory taste in the coffee, that and he was used to having his milk, obviously, refrigerated. But surprisingly it got him through the morning just fine. But for dinner, though, he was a Hemingway man. He needed a "clean, well-lighted place," one full of people even if he did eat alone. He wasn't anti-social or a recluse. He was simply too busy to cultivate casual relationships, but that didn't mean he shunned company.

He walked across the narrow street to the double doors of the building across the way, and then he climbed the four flights of stairs to the office. The door was already unlocked, which was good because he still didn't have a key, and Jill was making a pot of coffee when he came in.

She glanced up and said, "We take turns with the coffee. Next week will be your turn. Don't make it too strong."

Grant placed on his desk a battered leather briefcase he'd carried with him from his room. He paused a moment to admire Jill. She had her jacket off, a gray one today, and he could see that she had an admirable figure, all woman. Her hair was down, reaching the middle of her back. The hair had a luster to it: richness was a term that could be applied to all of her body. Full breasts, nice face, good complexion, pretty eyes, engaging smile, good mind ... she hadn't come up short in any one area that he could tell.

She glanced back at him, apparently aware of his appraisal. She blushed just a little, and then she recovered quickly and said, "Dale won't like your clothes."

The door opened as she said it, and Dale walked in, saying as he did, "She's right. You're not wearing a tie."

Grant was wearing gray slacks, a white, crewneck shirt,

and a navy blue sports coat. "We have a dress code?" he asked. "I don't remember seeing anything in the job description, other than clothing appropriate for work."

"A tie is appropriate," Dale said, shutting the door and carrying his own briefcase to his desk.

Grant opened his satchel, and, as the other two watched, he removed his sports coat and draped it over an arm, and then he pulled out a camera and hung it by its strap around his neck. Next he pushed up the sleeves of his shirt and finished the transformation by putting on a pair of sunglasses from the satchel. When he was done, he asked, "What do you see?"

Jill was the first to get it. "An incredible transformation that took about a minute."

"Exactly. If I were wearing a shirt and tie, the tie alone would be a dead giveaway even if I took off the coat. Being able to change your appearance quickly comes in very handy in police work."

Dale wasn't as impressed. "I still want to see you in a tie."

Grant didn't say anything. He had no intention of wearing a tie. He hadn't taken this job without learning something about it. This little office fell under the direction of the Assistant Legal Attaché in the embassy. They were here in part because the embassy had no room for them, and in part because the embassy wanted them someplace else, someplace away from it where they could send irritated Americans.

Dale was the contact person between their office and the embassy, but he was not technically the man in charge. Herbert Ingrahm was; he was the Assistant Legal Attaché. In reality, even the Legal Attaché, Mark Trumbo, wasn't in charge of Grant because, hired as a civil servant, he could not be fired by the FBI. He had to be fired by the State

Department as one of its civil servants. The whole process, because of the nature of the odd chain of command, was convoluted and time-consuming. Grant would probably have long tired of the job by the time someone in charge could get around to telling him he had to wear a tie or face termination.

"What's happening with the murders?" Grant asked.

Jill smiled. She knew that Dale was going to be in for a tough time when it came to Grant. He could lean on her hard enough to make her move, but he wasn't going to be able to do that with Grant.

Dale answered the question with a grunt. "Who the hell knows," he said.

Jill said, "We faxed the embassy the report we wrote up. No one's gotten back to us. Today we have a Mr. Wilbert coming in to demand to know why we haven't found his car yet. He and his family flew to Germany from Iowa, bought a top-of-the-line Mercedes directly from the plant, and then planned to tour Europe in it for a month before shipping it back to the States. This was to have been Mr. Wilbert's dream vacation, one he had planned in infinite detail for over a dozen years. Unfortunately, two days ago his Mercedes was stolen from the parking garage of his hotel."

"It's probably back in Germany being sold to another American even as we speak," Dale said.

"A Mrs. Todd Lashley-Heights will be in to find out why we have yet to locate her dog for her, the one that she let off the leash in the park below the Eiffel Tower."

"A police officer probably shot it when he caught the dog pooping on sacred Parisian grass," Dale said.

"We also have a couple coming in who had their passports stolen. This one we will take seriously," Jill said. "We'll get all the information we can, and then we'll send it directly to Interpol. With any luck we'll make the passports useless in a short time."

"Will we be doing any more with the murders?" Grant asked.

"Who knows?" Dale said, shaking his head. "Sometimes the embassy has us running all over hell for one of these things, and sometimes they slam the door on us and we never hear another word."

"What do you want me to do today?" Grant asked.

"Watch," Jill said. "Considering what we have to put up with during a typical day, I think we deserve the title of diplomat."

"When are these people due?" Grant asked.

She shrugged. "Tourists in the summer swarm about the city, which is why the locals prefer spring and fall. Sometimes they never show up, having had their vent at the embassy and their attention pulled away by museums, monuments, and parks. We get the ones who are still angry the next day."

The phone rang. Dale answered it, listened for a moment, and then indicated with a nod that the call was for Grant. "Inspector Gerard," he said, the expression on his face suggesting that he was not pleased that the French cop was calling Grant.

Grant took the call. He spoke with Gerard for nearly twenty minutes, noting with interest that both Jill and Dale feigned little interest in the call, but at the same time neither of them seemed to be doing much at their desks but listening to his end of the conversation.

As soon as he hung up, Dale was the first to ask. "What'd he want?"

Grant had written some notes in a little spiral notebook he always carried with him, and he finished penciling in a comment before answering the question. When he glanced up, he could see that Dale was about to explode from impatience. He managed to suppress a smile, more than likely a sure trigger to the explosion.

"He wanted me to know that I was right. Each of the victims had a third wound in the roof of the mouth. He fed the forensics information into Interpol, and the Assassin's profile came back."

"Lucky guess on your part," Dale said.

Grant looked hard at the man until Dale squirmed a little. Grant did not tolerate petty jealousies in the workplace. When he was promoted to head of detectives in Boston, he transferred two men just because of that. Dale wouldn't be as easy to move, but Grant would see to it that they worked as a team or one of them would go quickly.

"I find that luck is rarely a factor in anything, and when it is, it's a two-sided coin. You have a fifty percent chance of it running against you. When the Assassin did the tap in Boston, I started looking for anything I could find out about him. That wasn't much because he is very good at what he does."

"No one can be that good," Dale said, dismissing the idea with a roll of his eyes.

"The Assassin is. He gets paid a million dollars a pop, or that's the word on the street. He's a legend in organized crime, although I've never dealt with anyone who could even confirm a second- or even a third-party contact."

"Who'd pay a million bucks when you can buy a hit for a few thousand?" Jill asked.

"Someone who wants a guarantee of two things: first, that the hit will happen, and second, that it will never come back to stick on them. Since we don't know who the Assassin is, we can't stick a crime to him, which means we can't stick a hired hit on anyone else. That's what the folks who can afford it buy for a million bucks: murder with a guarantee."

"You were talking with Gerard about the location of hits," Dale said. "What was that all about?"

"Some of what Interpol has as a database on the Assassin came from me. I made him my private project when I was a homicide detective, and I wrote more than a few papers about him when I was working on my law degree. I was telling Gerard that I always thought that France might be the killer's home, because he never tapped anyone in this country."

"I guess that makes you wrong," Dale said.

"I thought so too, but Gerard pointed out that this is the first hit attributed to the Assassin since Boston. We decided that he might be hard up enough for cash that he was willing to break a rule about killing someone in his own country."

"That seems to be a lot of ifs," Jill said.

Grant smiled and leaned back in his chair, saying, "Yes, but isn't it pretty to think so?"

"Isn't that something out of Hemingway?" Jill asked.

Dale pushed away from his desk and stood up. "Before you wander off into literary lala-land, while I have the time I want to go over log-on procedures with Grant. You need to learn some codes and establish your own password to get into the computers at Interpol. You also need to learn the procedures for the secure phone line to the embassy. And you will be responsible for protecting any information you have, so we need to go over the procedures for that."

"I thought that procedure was already established," Grant said.

For a second Dale looked confused. "I haven't gone over this with you yet."

"I don't have a key to the door," Grant said. "Without it I can't get to either the computers or the telephone."

Dale looked relieved. He had been forgetful on occasion.

Forgetting to give Grant a key was one thing, but to forget a security briefing would have been far worse. "We have a safe in the next room. The keys are in it, as is a laptop computer and a cell phone for your personal use. You will need to protect that computer with your life. The desktop computers have pullout hard drives. If we leave the office unattended during the day and when we leave at night, we pull out the drives and lock them in the safe."

Grant had seen the safe through the windows from his room. It was large, perhaps six feet tall, and it looked like it weighed thousands of pounds. "I have an ID that was issued to me, but I understand that I will need to wear a security badge when I'm in the embassy. Where do I get that?"

"You'll get that at the Legat Office in the embassy. I'll send you over in a little while to do that. Someone will have to meet you at the door and escort you in. The embassy is a pretty secure place."

Grant followed Dale into the other room. The safe was against the back wall. It was a new model, and it had a keypad for punching in a code to open it. Dale told Grant the code, saying, "Memorize it. I don't want it written down anywhere. You get three tries to punch in the code, and then, if you get it wrong, a silent alarm goes out to the embassy. Security people will be here within five minutes."

"And the police?" Grant asked.

"Only as a last resort."

Dale opened the double doors to the safe. The first thing that caught Grant's eye when the doors opened was a 9MM automatic pistol in a leather shoulder holster. A box of shells sat beside it. "I thought you said no guns," Grant said.

"Two more of these are in the bottom drawer of the safe.

We are each issued one, but they stay in the safe. The only time we would use them is if the security of this office were threatened." He turned to Grant and repeated the words again. "*Only* if the security of the office is threatened are you to ever touch one of these guns."

Grant nodded. "Tell me about the laptop," he said.

Grant sat at one of the chairs to the conference table and spent the next half hour listening to lectures. The first was about the laptop. Grant was never to forget that it was easy to steal and difficult to make secure. He was encouraged to keep sensitive information on the office computer and not on the laptop. Like the cell phone, he said, both pieces of equipment used a network that scrambled signals, but a dedicated technician could find a way around all the security protections. Again, he was cautioned to use the cell phone to make arrangements for face-to-face communications and to use the laptop for writing reports and downloading research information he might need, but he should not save anything on the hard drive that needed to be kept secure.

The next lecture was on the organization of Legal Attaché Offices. These offices were manned by FBI agents who were given the titles of Legal Attaché, Deputy Legal Attaché, and Assistant Legal Attaché. The FBI had forty-four Legat Offices and four sub-offices in countries outside of the United States. The mission of the Legats was to deter crime that threatened America, such as drug trafficking, to combat international terrorism, and to blunt economic espionage. The agents also helped foreign police forces with training activities, and they used their offices to facilitate the resolution of domestic investigations that were international in scope.

Grant listened patiently to the lectures, but he wasn't giving them that much attention. He was not a man to take a job without understanding for whom he worked, what he was to do, and how he was to do it. He knew the organization of a Legat Office as well as Dale did.

What he did want to know, though, was how Dale saw his job, and how he saw his relationship with the Legat Office in Paris. Since, at least for now, Grant would have to go through Dale to get to the embassy, he thought it was important to understand Dale.

After the lectures, he was sent to the embassy to get his badge and to fill out forms for tax deductions and for health insurance. The rest of the afternoon was spent being given a tour of the Legat facilities and the embassy, and then being given one more time the whole series of lectures.

Bored stiff by the end of the workday, he called back to the office to let Dale know what had become of him. Jill informed him that he had gotten the best of it. Dale had gone to police headquarters to see if he could find out any more about the murders, leaving Jill to deal with the angry American with the missing Mercedes. The man had spent most of the afternoon in the office trying to look down her blouse when he wasn't blustering about the waste of taxpayers' money.

Grant did not return to the office. He'd left the laptop in the safe before he went to the embassy, and he had activated his cell phone so he could be reached if necessary. He walked from the embassy back to his hotel, stopping at the Cathédrale de Notre Dame, first to light two candles and then to kneel in a pew in the back to recite prayers for the dead.

SIX

He knew as soon as he read the article in the newspaper that he would be receiving a phone call. He was in his atrium pinching off dead leaves from his tropical plants and watering his small collection of orchids when his cell phone rang. He moved to a wicker chair located in a brilliant shaft of sunlight before he took the call, fixing his eyes on the Eiffel Tower in the distance. At his feet curled his Scottish Terrier, Rikki. Seated comfortably with his silver pot filled with fresh brewed coffee next to him, he answered with, "I was expecting to hear from you."

The voice. That was what he called the man on the other end of the line. They had never met formally. Neither wanted to meet. They arranged business deals over this very private phone line. The voice said, "I've some very unhappy customers."

"I thought that might be the case when I saw the story."

"The arrangement was for the one, not the other."

Even though the phone was safe, neither of them would ever say the kinds of words that would convict them of a murder. He made "arrangements" to handle a "client" for a "customer." The customer had been satisfied, the client taken care of, but the complication of the second death had everyone worried. To kill one person connected to a powerful person was risky enough, but to kill a second connected to another powerful person was dangerous. FBI, Interpol,

French police, South American security agencies ...
his slight indiscretion had brought a lot of forces into
play.

"Excusez-moi!" he said. "I followed the client for three
days before I got an opportunity. Unfortunately, when I got
my opening, she was not alone. I was not able to separate
one from the other, so I had to do both. I was told that time
was an issue ..." He let that trail off. He had gone without
work for two years, and he was beginning to feel the financial pinch because of it. He could not afford for them to
place the blame of this mess on his shoulders alone.

In reality he knew the blame rested with him. He'd been
living the good life for too long and he had enjoyed the
chance to be out of the business for a while. He might even
have made it a permanent retirement if it had not been for
the stock market. Yes, he had made a great deal of money
during the last decade, but not as much as some people
suspected. It took him years to build a reputation, and it
wasn't until he had that did the big money start rolling in.
On the street it was said he was paid a million dollars for
what he did, but that was street folklore. He actually got
paid about €800,000, and that was only later. In the beginning he was lucky to get a tenth of that.

With the increased reward came an improved lifestyle.
He lived well; compensation, he thought, for what he did.
He was not a man without conscience. He needed something to assuage the guilt feelings that came with the job.
Good living seemed to do the trick. Good living, though,
was now threatened. The market had cut deeply into his
principal. He had less to live on now, and one arrangement
in two years certainly wasn't going to replace what he had
lost.

He would not explain any of this to the Voice, because
he knew that man would not care. He cared only about two

things: that the job be done right, and that none of it ever came back at him. They all shared that in common.

The job had not been done right. He had hurried it because ... he had to face the truth. He had lost patience. The silly children wanted to play all night long. By two in the morning he only wanted to be home and in bed, sleeping peacefully between his silk sheets. He did not want to spend another late night out tracking the client, looking for that narrow window of opportunity. So he took out both of them. How was he to know that they were both connected, and the customer only had leverage with one of the connections?

"Everyone is more worried about consequences than they are about blame at the moment. I've been told to have you stand by in case more needs to be done. We may have other clients for you, but I'm afraid you can expect a severe discount being applied as punishment."

"I'm not going anywhere," he said.

"Keep your phone turned on at all times."

The call ended and he turned off the cell phone, shoving it into the pocket of a smoking jacket. Discount? He wouldn't do it. Why put his life in danger without appropriate incentive? He had only walked back to his orchids before he reconsidered. A penthouse with an atrium in the heart of Paris was a luxury that few could afford. Without additional income or a remarkable change in the stock market, he would not be able to afford it much longer. He reached into his pocket and pulled out the phone, turning it back on and punching in the code so that it was ready to receive calls.

SEVEN

After his trip to the church, and after he had a dinner of venison with blackberry sauce in a restaurant at la place St-Michel, Grant went back to the office. As he opened the door with his key, he was still contemplating his full belly and his light wallet. The meal prices were something he had to get used to in Paris.

He disarmed the security system with the code he had been given, and opened the safe on the first try. He turned on his computer and logged on to Interpol without a hitch. He considered himself a modern cop. He could do all of these things with ease.

He ran two names, Tiffany Sutherby and Escobar Saldano. Tiffany's name did not come up. Escobar had a small file. He was fond of fast cars and fast speeds. He'd caused enough problems in several countries to warrant a note in an Interpol file.

Tiffany's grandfather's name was Walter Sutherlin. Grant turned to the Internet to see what he could find out about him. He found out quite a bit. Sutherlin was the son of a man who had done very well in oil, and then he had done even better in stocks, buying them up by the basketful when the stock market collapsed in America in 1929. Like a very few, very lucky people, he had guessed right, that what went down would eventually come up. Financial planners for the family continued through the years to make the right decisions for the family fortune, turning hundreds of millions into billions. Walter Sutherlin's role, it appeared, was to oversee the family fortune, which meant he kept tabs on the financial planners. Watching money could not have been very hard work, Grant thought.

Grant next did the tedious task of searching out public records in New York City and New York State to find out what he could about Tiffany Sutherby. An hour later he had found enough to know that she wasn't an innocent child, and, he suspected that if he could find this out from public records that the private one was probably far worse. For every traffic ticket, DUI, and possession of a controlled substance that showed up, he would guess as many more had been "handled" by the family.

Tiffany liked alcohol and she liked drugs. She also liked to party under the influence of both. Twice she had been picked up in raids on parties that had gotten out of hand. Three times she had been arrested while driving under the influence. One case involving her had referred to "several" DUI arrests.

He went back on the Internet to see if he could get to any records in Bolivia that might refer to Escobar, but, as he suspected, nothing came up. His father was a powerful man. He had the resources to keep such things out of public records.

He shut down the computer and put his hard drive back in the safe. Before he closed the safe, he pulled out the automatic from its holster and looked at it. He dropped the clip from the handle to confirm that the gun was loaded. He worked the slide and ejected a 9MM shell. The gun was ready for business. He checked the two in the drawer at the bottom of the safe and found them both loaded and ready to go as well. He put the guns back as they were and locked the safe.

He turned off the lights in the office, but instead of leaving he went to his desk and sat down. With his hands behind his head, leaning against the wall, and his feet on the desktop, he considered what he had found out.

Either the boy or the girl might have been the target. Either one could have gotten into something they shouldn't have, probably to do with drugs. Either could have been used to send a message to a parent or a grandparent.

A million dollar message, though? He focused on that figure for a moment. He had never believed it. A competent hit could be bought for a lot less. A discreet hit could be bought for a tenth of that, a twentieth. What if the million wasn't in dollars but some other currency? Not pounds. That would make it even more than a million dollars. What about Euro? If the man lived in France then Euro would be right. That would make it about $851,000. That, too, was high for a top-of-the-line type of hit, but Grant always thought that the Assassin lived in Paris, he'd never made a hit in France. That fact stood out and gnawed at Grant.

What then could Tiffany or Escobar have been into to be worth that kind of money? Or what might a relative be into? Most crime had at its heart one common factor: money. A high-price hit would mean that a heck of a lot of money was at stake. That usually meant drugs, but drugs didn't feel right. Both of these kids came from wealthy families. He didn't see the motivation for them to get into the kind of drug trafficking that would lead to big money. If he were to make a guess right now, he would have to guess that it was something else. He didn't have a clue as to what that something else might be.

First, though, he would have to eliminate drugs as the motivation for the hit.

The phone on his desk rang, startling him. If he'd felt

any guilt about what he was doing, he would have let it ring. He felt no guilt. He was doing his job as he defined it. He answered the phone. "Grant," he said.

"I thought it would be you," Jill said. "I got a call from the security at the embassy asking me if I knew who might be back in the office."

"I'm surprised they didn't call Dale," Grant said.

"They did, but he wasn't in. He likes to go out at night for a drink and a chance to get lucky."

Grant laughed. "He doesn't seem like the type."

"From my observations, he's usually hungover and unlucky. I do worry, though, because I know his habits are known in the embassy, and some folks there are concerned that he might get picked up by an operative."

"The cold war is over," he said. "We won."

"That only means that everybody has freed up more people to spy on everyone else. We're always looking for an edge; so is everyone else. So what are you doing?"

"Playing with my new toys."

"I thought you went for the simple life."

"I can afford to do that when I get to play with other people's toys."

"You haven't answered my question."

For the first time Grant wondered if Jill thought she was in charge in the office, not Dale. "Are you sure the embassy called Dale first?"

He thought he heard a soft chuckle. "You were doing …?"

"Cruising the net to see what I could find out about Sutherby and Saldano."

"And?"

"They probably spent a lot of time standing in the corner when they were growing up."

"Not angels, then."

"No, but not devils either. A little wild maybe."

"I wouldn't bring it up tomorrow unless the information is offered."

"Bring it up where?"

"Mr. and Mrs. Sutherby will be arriving to make funeral arrangements for their daughter's body. They want to talk to the 'investigator in charge,' which everyone has ingloriously decided is you. A man with a few billion dollars scares the crap out of diplomats, especially when he's a friend of the president. You're new; you're expendable. What do you think about that?"

"I'd have been disappointed if they'd named anyone else."

"I thought so. You're going to be a problem, aren't you?"

"Are you talking about work or play?"

"Both," she said.

"I'm grinning," he said.

"Nothing here is going to be as easy as you think it is. Call the embassy and let them know that you're packing it up for the night and going home. You have a long day tomorrow."

"Is that an order?"

"Motherly advice."

"I don't need mothering."

"Yes you do," she said. "You just don't know it yet." She hung up.

He called the embassy and then shut up the office for the night. He wasn't surprised that the office was monitored. That's the way he would have done it. He liked the idea that he worked with people who did things the way he would do them.

He returned to his room and sat in a comfortable armchair he had purchased and placed near the French windows. With his feet on an ottoman that came with the chair, he relaxed with his headset on, listening to a CD of soft jazz music, while he reread Hemingway's *A Moveable Feast*. He was curious to learn how Paris had changed since Hemingway had lived here in the 1920s.

The chair was too comfortable. He woke up to the morning's light with the headsets still on and the book by Hemingway folded closed in this lap. He pulled off the headsets and put them on the desk next to the chair. Tentatively, he tested his muscles. He expected to be stiff from sleeping in a sitting position. He slowly pushed himself from the chair and found that he wasn't as sore as he thought he would be, but he felt groggy, as if he hadn't gotten the deep sleep he needed.

His body was probably worried about falling out of the chair, he told himself. It must have spent the night holding on for dear life. He still had a half hour before he needed to get up. He moved to the bed and stretched out. His alarm was set, so he allowed himself to drift off to sleep.

He woke up twenty-nine minutes later, just in time to roll over and turn off the alarm before it sounded. This time, as he sat up, he felt much better. He felt frisky enough to get up and head for the shower. The shower would kick-start the day. Even with enough sleep, he couldn't get going full speed in the mornings without a hot shower first.

A half hour later he was letting himself into the office, the first one to get there. He was working on his laptop when Jill came in. He glanced up at her, and then he did a double take. Again she was wearing a skirt with a suit coat to match, but under the coat she had on a stretch top that was form fitting. In case he might have missed it the first time, she took off the coat, took a hanger from a coat rack near the door, and then hung it up.

She did indeed have breasts, he noted. The top was snug

enough that it swelled her breasts, so that he was given a view of a little cleavage. She walked to her desk and sat down, acting as if nothing today was different from any other day. But today was different, he told himself. Today he saw cleavage. Yesterday he had not.

"What are you working on?" she asked.

"I'm making some notes to myself about what I've learned so far about the double homicide. I wanted to write down what I saw at the crime scene while it was still fresh in my mind."

"Why the laptop? You've got a desktop computer," she said.

"I like the mobility," he said. What he didn't add was he also liked the security. He'd drop all this information onto disks, and then he would wipe the computer clean. He suspected that if the Attaché's Office could monitor this office, even at night, and even with the alarm off, then they could monitor the desktop computers as well. For now he didn't want anyone knowing what he was doing. The owner of the hotel had a small safe for his guest's personal items. Grant had already made an arrangement to keep some things in it, including his disks.

"The parents will be in at ten," Jill said. "Don't expect to see Dale until they're long gone. He doesn't like emotional situations."

"What can you tell me about the parents?"

Jill reached into her purse and pulled out a little notebook. He liked the idea that she kept information like he did.

She read from her notes. "Tiffany Sutherby was the granddaughter of Walter Sutherlin. Her mother is Margaret Sutherlin Sutherby, and she is the second daughter of three fathered by Walter. She brought money into the marriage. Her husband, Scott Sutherby, brought education. He has a Ph.D. in economics. As best I can tell, Tiffany's parents don't do a whole lot. Scott will likely be asked to manage his father-in-law's fortune, but not all of it. Walter apparently has some reservations. I think those reservations might have something to do with the amount of time that Scott spends on the tennis court or the golf course."

"We know that Walter has some impressive connections. What about Scott and Margaret?" Grant asked.

"I suspect that if they carried the weight that Walter carries, they wouldn't be dealing with us. Someone in the embassy would be holding their hands."

This was the part of police work that Grant disliked the most: dealing with the parents of victims. He had his own feelings about people who had been murdered. Never though could his feelings match those of the parents. On different emotional levels, it was as if they did not speak the same language. More of a defense mechanism than anything else, he always resorted to professionalism to get him through it. He would say the right things and do the right things, but he would want nothing more than for it to be over.

The door opened and the Sutherbys walked in. Grant did not have time to slip on his jacket before the two stopped in front of his desk. "Agent Reynolds?" Mrs. Sutherby asked.

He stood and extended his hand to both of them. Scott Sutherby returned a firm handshake, while Margaret Sutherby simply let her fingers slip through his. "I'm not an agent," he said, "but a field representative."

"You were at the scene of my daughter's murder?" Mrs. Sutherby asked.

"Yes."

"Then I want you to tell me everything about it."

Grant knew that grief came in lots of different forms.

He could see it in the tightness around Mr. Sutherby's eyes. He looked like a pleasant man, one who was probably quick to smile according to the creases around his mouth. He was tall and handsome, but when Grant looked at Mrs. Sutherby he thought of Scott as the sperm donor, because the gene pool for the daughter came from the wife. Mother and daughter looked alike. They could even be sisters, but with a keen detective's eye, Grant could see where the skin had been nipped and tucked on Mrs. Sutherby's face. The appearance of youth had come at a very high price charged by an expensive plastic surgeon.

Plastic surgeons could do wonders with the face and other parts of the body, but where their magic could not reach were the hands and arms. He could see her age in the transparent skin on the back of the hands, and in the fine, spider-web crosshatching of lines on the back of her arms. Youth had slipped by, but she was still trying to live by the memory of it.

"Let's go into the conference room." He had a feeling this wasn't going to be pleasant. He escorted the two of them into the back room, and then he held up a hand to indicate to Jill not to join them. With a thumb, he gestured to himself. He would take it. He closed the door.

Scott Sutherby had taken a seat at the table, but Mrs. Sutherby remained standing, and she chose a spot so that Grant had little choice but to come to a stop in front of her.

"I want to know what you saw."

He had seen this look in a woman's eyes before. This woman got what she wanted. Diplomacy wasn't going to work with her, so he went right to professionalism.

"While walking down a narrow alley a few blocks from here at some time after two in the morning, your daughter was shot in the back of the head at close range by what appears to be a single gunman. As she was falling to the ground, she caused the man she was with, Escobar Saldano, to bend down slightly as they were walking arm in arm and her arm pulled him down. He, then, was also shot in the back of the head at close range.

"The gun was silenced. Even Saldano, shot second, was apparently not aware that your daughter had been shot. By the position of his body, the expression on his face, and the fixing of the eyes—although none of these is an exact science—he appeared never to have known what was happening.

"Your daughter went down and then he fell on top of her. Since neither of the victims, each ultimately shot three times, bled much, I suspect that their hearts stopped beating soon after the first shot. There was no indication that your daughter moved after she dropped. She did not try to drag herself; her arms and legs were in the position they should be in if she simply dropped to the ground."

She stared intently into Grant's eyes. He saw in the eyes, too late, the searing anger. Her hand came up fast and with enough momentum so that when it connected to his face, Grant was staggered by the blow. She reached back to slap him again, but he caught her hand high, before it could come around.

"I don't believe it is wise, Mrs. Sutherby," he said, his own eyes boring into hers, "that you assault a federal agent, FBI or not."

Scott Sutherby stirred uncomfortably in his chair, but he did not try to get up. He said, feebly, "Dear, that's not going to change anything."

They stayed like that for several seconds, locked in an awkward pose, their arms extended, his hand still clasping her wrist. "I didn't kill your daughter, Mrs. Sutherby, nor am I sure of who did, or why. You need to redirect your anger."

Finally the tension went out of her arm. He lowered her arm back to her side, but he remained light on his feet, ready to deflect another blow if necessary.

It wasn't. She slowly eased herself into a chair next to her husband. Grant did not sit. He wanted his size hovering over the two of them subconsciously to intimidate them. He wanted honest answers before they had time to gather their emotions and let reason take over.

"Do you know of any reasons why someone would have your daughter killed?" he asked.

The two exchanged a brief glance, and then Margaret answered. "No."

"Your daughter had some problems in the past with drugs. Could it have been drug related?"

She shook her head no, but her eyes showed a hint of doubt. He pushed the question. "I'm not talking about recreational use. All indications are that this was a professional hit to kill either your daughter or Saldano. For this kind of a hit, we would be talking about large sums of money and large quantities of drugs."

This time the doubt was not in her eyes. "No. Tiffany may have experimented more than some children with drugs, but she had more money than most children. She had so much money, she wouldn't have needed to deal in drugs at all. She could afford the kind of lifestyle that selling drugs can offer without the risks. Despite what you may have read in her police records, Tiffany wasn't that much of a risk-taker."

"What about this Saldano guy?" Scott asked.

"The son of a diplomat. Playful to the point of troublesome, but not a hell-raiser. So far we see nothing in his background that would explain a professional hit."

"Could it have been a mistake?" Margaret asked.

"Professional hits like this are almost never a mistake.

The people who carry them out are very, very good at what they do, which means they don't get sloppy." He sat down in a chair on the other side of the table from them. "When nothing jumps off the page when I'm looking at the victims, I have to step back. I have to look at the people closest to the victims to see if the reason might be there instead of with the victims."

"Are you suggesting that this might have something to do with Margaret and myself?" Grant was impressed. Scott was as sharp as his credentials said he was.

"Or further," Grant said. He turned his attention back to Margaret. "Your father is a billionaire. Billionaires sometimes step on toes to get where they are, or they sometimes incite resentment or jealousy. Could this have something to do with your father?"

Grant saw the spark in her eyes and then the anger come back, but this time she held it in check, only turning slightly to make that brief eye contact with her husband. He lowered his head. Even if something wasn't directly connected to Walter Sutherlin, Grant was sure the two of them thought it might be.

"Can you give me any ideas?"

Mrs. Sutherby stood up and lifted her purse from the table. She clutched it to her body and walked to the door. She paused there to slip the strap of the purse over her shoulder and to reach out to rest a hand on the doorknob. These were carefully orchestrated actions, Grant noticed, designed to distract from what was really going on. What was really going on was that she was in a struggle to decide if she should tell him something. He didn't care how much education she had, how much money, or how much sophistication, she could hide this struggle no better than a prostitute trying to decide to rat on a pimp or a druggy trying to decide if he should rat on his dealer.

The battle came to a quick end. She turned the handle on the door. "We must go. We have to make arrangements to ship our daughter back home."

Scott got up and followed her out the door. He mumbled as he walked by Grant, "Should we think of anything ..." He let the words trail off.

They were already closing the office door behind them when Grant reached the conference room door. Jill sat at her desk and stared at him. "I heard her slap your face, even from in here with the door closed. Did you see it coming?"

"I saw something coming—some explosion. That's one angry woman. If I had thought it was going to be a slap, it never would have happened."

"You have a nice command voice," she said. "'It's not wise to assault a federal agent,'" she said, trying to mimic Grant's voice.

"Was I that loud?"

She pointed to the computer speakers on her desk. "The room is wired for sound. We can pick up and record whatever goes on in there on our computers. I recorded your interview. I guess I should have told you."

He smiled. "Let me guess," he said. "You did it so you could come to my rescue if need be."

"No," she said, "I did it because you are the new guy and you're probationary, and somewhere down the line you will be evaluated on how you do your job. This is the first piece of evidence for that evaluation."

"And?"

"You're good," she said. "So now what do you think about the deaths?"

"I think Margaret thinks daddy has something to do with it, but what I think is meaningless without some evidence to support it. Saldano could have been the target, but at least now I know that something buried in the Sutherlin family could be the reason for the deaths. At least the parents think so."

"What now?"

"I need to learn everything I can about Walter Sutherlin. I doubt there's much that Margaret and her husband do that he doesn't control." In his best western drawl, he said, "The man's got a powerful lot of money, and with a powerful lot of money comes a powerful lot of power."

Jill laughed. As her smile faded, the expression on her face turned to something else. She wasn't a woman to openly lust for a man, but sometimes she couldn't help it. She knew she had this expression that resembled a mother watching her sleeping child. It was a look full of satisfaction and pleasure. That's what she felt when she looked at Grant. "Can I take you to lunch?" she asked.

He leaned in the doorframe and watched that look, wondering what it meant. "Sure," he said.

EIGHT

Dale spent the morning at the embassy, leaving Jill and Grant alone in the office. Dale called once to tell them that they could close up the office for lunch, but they were to make sure to take their cell phones with them, and they were to be back no later than one. He had some work for them to do.

Grant spent the morning learning how to do the paperwork. Filling out forms might seem easy to an outsider, but Grant knew that agencies, whether civilian or governmental, had a way that the paperwork was to be done. It was no different working for the government even stationed in Paris.

After that, he studied up on protocol. Although it was okay, he learned, for him to call Inspector Gerard on his own because this was his direct contact involving a crime against an American, it was not okay for him to contact directly anyone higher up than the inspector. He was to contact the office of the Assistant Legal Attaché, who, in turn, would route the request to someone in the embassy. The embassy official who actually made the contact would depend on the rank of the person to be contacted. If Grant needed to talk to someone high enough up in the French government, the ambassador to France himself would make the contact. Then the request would work its way back down the ladder on the French side, until someone in the government equal to Grant's rank would contact him.

When he started to say something to Jill about this cumbersome process, she held up her hand and said, "Don't say another word. I've lived with this for over a year. A lot of our work is simply waiting for someone to return our request for a call. Don't ever, though, circumvent the system. The French already think that American diplomats are uncivilized as it is. An indiscretion in diplomatic decorum will get you sent home faster than anything else."

With an interesting murder case dropping into his lap on his first day at work, and with the pleasure of staying in Paris, Grant wasn't about to do anything that would get him sent home in a hurry. On the other hand, he had already tagged Interpol as the best source of information for him. His security clearance gave him access to all the records he needed, and he had discovered that a request through Interpol could put him in contact with these records faster than his own embassy could. Interpol could cut through red tape.

They closed up the office a little before noon. She led him up le boulevard St-Michel, away from the river, to a small café several blocks from the office. Like most cafés in this section of town, it had some sidewalk seating, but she took him inside. "You'll like this," she said.

He decided that it was Jill who was going to get the kick out of this. As soon as they walked in the café, two large German shepherd dogs came to greet them at the door, both obviously friends of Jill's. "Can you believe it," she said, squatting down so the dogs could lick her face, "that they allow dogs in a restaurant?"

The dogs quickly moved to the next customer coming into the café, and Jill and Grant worked their way through a lunch crowd to a small table next to the front windows. "This is my favorite seat in the whole place," Jill said. "I love enjoying a leisurely European style lunch while watching the people walk by."

After scanning the menu, they both selected the fruit and cheese plate, with a cup of garlic soup. And, in true French fashion, Jill ordered wine for them both. Grant wasn't surprised that Jill started the conversation with the question he'd expected as soon as they'd settled down to eat. He'd been asked it often.

"Be honest now," she said. "Tell me how you've managed to make it to your mid-thirties without being married."

"Good living," he said.

She made a face at him. "Be serious," she said.

"Like the typical American male, I was brought up to believe that a man should be married, that he ought to date until he finds the right girl, that he should make sure first, and then he should marry her. Then he should have kids."

"So far so good," she said, between sips of soup.

"I was in no position to get married while I was going to college or while I was in the military. Either I didn't have the money, or I didn't meet anyone that interesting, or I was on the move. It didn't take me long on the job, as a cop, to have some doubts about bringing kids into the world. I saw too many of them abused, tortured, or murdered."

"We'll call that," she said, "if you forgive the pun, a cop out."

"Okay, but it was part of the equation. I believed then that you had to find someone you liked, you had to date her long enough to know if you loved her, and when you found that out, then you needed to work on a relationship, and, if all went well, you got married. That didn't happen while I was on the beat. I dated, I got involved, but love ..." He shrugged.

"Okay. That gets you to your late twenties. That still gives you plenty of time to get married." She reached across the table and pulled a slice of melon from his plate. "You don't need this," she said.

"But it was nice of you to ask," he said, smiling.

"Fill me in on the next six years of your love life quickly, or I'll have to finish off that cheese and bread too."

He liked a trim woman who ate well. That meant she burned off calories in other ways. Some did it through extensive exercise programs, which Grant knew was not Jill's thing, and others did it with a hot furnace—a metabolic rate second to none. He had often found that women like that were the most interesting in bed.

"I've spent the last six years working as a homicide detective while going to law school. It took me longer than most to get my law degree, and the other full-time students were as busy as I was. We didn't have time for relationships. We did have time for sex, though. Wham, bam, thank you, ma'am, was the rule of the day."

"That sounds pretty callous," she said.

"Most lawyers are black-and-white thinkers. Callous falls in the gray area."

"And no one minded?"

"You can always find exceptions, but most of the people I knew in law school thought their futures began after they got their degree. Besides, I was a cop. Even as law students, they didn't quite trust me, especially when it came to their futures."

"And there was no one, special person?"

He smiled, but behind the smile was a bit of sadness. Two, maybe three times he might have gotten to the next level with a woman, one that could have led to marriage. Once it was with a fellow cop. She died in a shoot-out with bank robbers. He had been involved with another woman, an assistant DA, when he decided to take the job in Boston and start work on a law degree. The relationship did not survive the distance between them. And there was one in law school, but she was like a Tiffany Sutherby, from a social stratum alien to him. They had been involved at school, but it only took a weekend at her parents' house in the Hamptons for them both to know it wouldn't work.

"No," he said, "nothing serious. What about you? How come you're not married?"

She took her napkin from her lap and patted her lips, and then she folded it neatly and set it beside her plate. Anal, Grant wondered, or simply neat? She then lifted her wine glass and held it with both hands. "I love drinking in the afternoon—not drinking to get drunk, just a little glass to put you at ease. I love it that it's the social norm here."

"Why do I get the feeling that you're avoiding my question?"

She rested her elbows on the table and continued to cradle the wine glass. "Avoiding? No. Stalling? Yes. I'm trying to think of a good answer."

"How about the truth?"

"Okay, I'll go with Grant's truth: the right guy hasn't come along yet."

He laughed. "Is that my truth?"

"You tell me you've had women in your life, that you've been involved, but that you haven't fallen madly in love. That sounds pretty familiar to me. In fact, it sounds like you were talking about my life."

"No one guy that came even close?" he asked.

"I was raised by a mother taken with the feminist movement. Don't get me wrong. It wasn't for her, but she decided it was just the thing for her daughters. We were told over and over again not to get tied down too young, to get a good education so we'd always be able to take care of ourselves, taste a little bit of the world while we could, enjoy the chance to work outside the home. My father was a successful lawyer. My mother stayed at home and took care of us. All and all, it was a nice way to be raised. I always wondered why my mother didn't want it for my two sisters and myself."

"The grass is greener?"

"I guess," she said. "Mom always admired women who accomplished something with their lives through their art or through their careers."

"So you followed your mother's advice, and here you are suffering for it, stuck in Paris, working for the State Department, and making a good salary."

"I don't feel sorry for myself," she said. "I want my cake and eat it too. So far I've had my cake. I'm still waiting for the right guy to come along. I expect it to happen. And you?"

He finished his wine, set down the glass, and pulled his napkin from his lap and tossed it on his plate. "Finding love is like finding a clue to a crime. Without the clue, you aren't going to solve it. Without a woman ..." He stood up.

Reluctantly, she put down her glass, but before she could stand, her cell phone rang. She pulled it from her purse and answered it. She listened for a few moments, and then said, "We're coming back to the office now."

Grant picked up the check, leaving the money on the table. She followed. "Dale?" he asked.

"Yes," she said. "We have fifteen requests through the embassy to check on the welfare of some young Americans in Paris. The story of the murders has broken in the U.S., and now every parent who hasn't heard from his or her child in Paris is worried sick."

"That sounds like a pain in the butt," he said, as he paid for the lunch.

"It's not that bad. Most of the kids are staying in hotels, and the French will have a record of their whereabouts.

We just need to call the hotels and confirm that they are still there. The parents will have given us addresses for the rest. We'll probably be able to do it by phone. How's your French?"

"Not that great," he said.

She put her arm in his outside on the sidewalk, and said, as they walked back toward the office, "By the time you're done helping with these calls, you'll be damned near fluent."

NINE

He stood on an observation deck that overlooked Paris. The deck was perched on the top of a department store, and a circular stairway accessed it. The deck was circular as was the stone railing around it, and on the rail were plaques that identified each of the major buildings that could be seen in the distance in that particular direction. He came here often because it gave him a pleasant view of Paris, and it wasn't as crowded with tourists as the Eiffel Tower. He truly loved this city.

For that reason alone he had made a promise to himself that he would never take a job in Paris. Part of his success was his ability to pack up and leave town after he had killed someone. That made it so much more difficult for the police to get a handle on him.

He knew, logically, that he shouldn't be at any greater risk having killed someone in Paris than anywhere else, but that was the logical part of his brain. Another part of it harbored all of his fears, the greatest that he would lose all that he had earned for himself in this beautiful city.

He moved to the plaque that identified Ile de la Cite and the Cathédrale de Notre Dame. From here, if he could see beyond the cathedral, he would be able to look at the mouth of la Rue du Chat-Qui-Pêche. As he stood there, staring at something he could not see from here, he worried about what was becoming of him. He had never faltered before.

He had never shown weakness in his resolve to do what he set out to do. Why, then, had he given in and allowed himself to take this latest job? It violated everything he held strong. He took a job in his own backyard. He took a job because he needed money. He took a job because he was afraid that if he didn't, another one would not be offered. Weakness. Each reason showed weakness in him.

Weakness was what got a man captured. Weakness was what got a man killed. If any of his victims had shown even the least bit of caution, he or she might still be alive today. They were fools for being weak.

The fear of turning weak was not as great as the restlessness he now felt. In the past he was able to complete a job, leave, and put it behind him. The money was paid and the good life continued. He hated this waiting to see what would happen next. He hated being kept on hold, possibly being called upon to fix a job that others saw as botched. If he had been given enough information in the beginning, he wouldn't have killed the two of them, just the one. He wasn't the one to blame. They'd made the mistake and now they were trying to blame it on him.

He had been told that he was to make the hit to send a message. For the first time in two days, he allowed himself a slight smile. What the men who hired him did not know was that he knew who they were. They had gone to great lengths to keep that information from him, but they had made a mistake. They had hired a man who lived in the same city they lived in. He had killed nearly a dozen people before he found that out. He had kept the information to himself. He suspected that some day it might come in handy. The irony, of course, was they did not know who he was. He had created an elaborate number of precautions to keep them from knowing who he was, but the first two precautions proved to be the most valuable. He had murdered the man who had put them in contact with him, and then he had murdered the man who had made the contact with him. As he discovered over time, his name had never gone further than the two. He even knew who the Voice was.

Knowing who they were definitely had an advantage. Perhaps it was time for him to send them a message. He would make the message obvious enough so they would know it came from him. Then they would treat him with a little more respect.

TEN

Grant leaned against the windowsill of the office with a cup of coffee in hand and stared into his room across the alley. He actually wasn't seeing anything. He was focused on his thoughts instead. He was trying to figure out a way to trace the Assassin in the opposite direction he had tried before.

Before he had tried to follow the victim back to the killer. That had not worked. The Assassin simply was too good for that. The opposite direction was equally impossible. Start with five million Parisians and eliminate them one by one until he reached the Assassin. Lateral thinking. If you can't do it one way, try another. The trouble was that neither way would work. So what next?

He watched as a couple walked up the alley and entered a bar on the corner. This was the first chance he had to drink a cup of coffee and relax. An American businessman had been assaulted and robbed. The man was in critical condition in a hospital in Paris. The police weren't sure who had done it. Grant had gone over the details of the crime with Gerard, gone to the hospital to learn what he could about the man, been on the phone with the man's company in Chicago, and had contacted the nearest relatives back in the States. By the end of the day he was pretty sure the man had been picked up by a male prostitute and had been led into the alley where he had been beaten and robbed.

Gerard agreed. The problem was that the man, if a homosexual, was a closet one. He had a wife and kids back home, and he had a boss who couldn't think of any reason that the man might be singled out except as a target for robbery. Grant had finished the afternoon by writing up everything he had learned and sending it to the embassy. He liked that about the job. When it got sticky, he could pass it on to someone else to deal with it.

Jill joined him, leaning against the opposite side of the window with a cup of coffee in hand. Again Dale had set his own agenda. Some counterfeit U.S. currency was showing up in Paris and he was gathering information. He was going to Lyons tomorrow to the Interpol headquarters, and wasn't sure when he would be back.

Jill filled him in. Dale always took the cases that would allow him to travel on an expense account. He was known to take longer than he should, especially if it meant going to a city where he had not been before. Sometimes he disappeared for a week at a time, calling in every day from a new location. He got away with it because not only could he write thorough reports, but because he was damned good at justifying the trips and the expenses. She did note, too, that he took his camera with him. He loved playing the tourist.

"When do you think Dale will be back?" Grant asked.

She shrugged. "He's been to Lyons before. On the other hand, he did say the bills were showing up on the French Riviera. We may never see him again."

"Does that make you my boss while he's gone?"

She laughed. "No, Dale will call every day to remind us he's still the boss."

"What's next?"

"I'm caught up. You're caught up. We wait and see what shows up in the morning. Who knows, maybe Americans will stay out of trouble for a few days and we won't have much to do."

"If that's the case, would you mind if I took some time to see if I can find out anything more about the murders?"

"Would it make any difference how I answered that?" she asked.

He liked the fact that she asked questions like that without a trace of sarcasm. She seemed to really want to know the answer. He felt like she was trying to understand him without being judgmental. "If you objected strenuously, I'd do it on my own time."

"What do you intend to do?"

"Visit Gerard on his turf. Find out who at Interpol is the expert about the Assassin and talk to him personally. Do some deeper research into Walter Sutherlin and see if there's a secret buried in his closet."

She nodded her head. "Sounds good," she said. "I only have one stipulation."

"What's that?"

"You take me with you tomorrow, and you have dinner with me tonight."

"That's two stipulations."

Her eyes drifted up from her coffee cup, took in his shoulders for a moment, and then settled on his eyes. She held him in her gaze, bold and unblushing, and said, "I haven't gotten to the stipulation yet."

"Okay."

"Dinner will be at my place. I'll cook."

"I can live with that," he said. "Or at least I hope I can. You can cook?"

"Hey," she said. "This is Paris. You don't live in Paris for over a year without taking a few cooking classes."

"Would your mother approve?"

"She loves it. She's always dreamed of coming to Paris to

take a cooking class."

"That might make a nice birthday present for her."

She tilted her head slightly to one side, her eyes still locked on his and a smile slowly forming. "There's not a romantic buried in you someplace, is there? That's a lovely idea."

"My parents are dead," he said. "I'm always thinking of things I wished I'd done with them."

"I'm sorry," she said.

"Don't be," he said. "If you haven't figured it out yet, much of life is about loss."

She reached over and took his coffee cup from his hands. "I'll need to do some shopping for groceries. I'll give you directions to my place. Plan to show up about eight. In the meantime, you get to lock up."

Off the conference room was a small bathroom. She rinsed the cups in the sink, set them on a paper towel on the conference table to dry, and gathered up her things to leave. At the door she handed him a slip of paper with the directions, and then she left, saying as a parting shot, "Clean the coffeemaker and set it up for tomorrow."

After she left, he thought, "women." Always afraid they weren't in control. Always wanting to be in control. Always pretending they were. It didn't seem to matter how smart, or pretty, or educated they were. Control was big with the women he had known. He hoped Jill wasn't like that. He wasn't into controlling anyone, and he certainly wasn't one who would let himself be controlled.

But he did clean the coffeemaker and set it up for the next day before locking up. With a few hours of light left in the day, he decided to walk. He had nothing in particular he wanted to see. Paris, packed full of sights as small as a plaque commemorating war dead to the massive Musée de Louvre, held some interest for him, and he would see each in time, but for now he simply enjoyed absorbing the ambiance of this wonderful city. For no reason he could explain, walking these streets made him feel like a part of the history of man instead of just another isolated event.

While he walked, he thought about Jill. She had made no promises to him other than a dinner, but he felt the electricity between them. This was no large jolt, but it was a symbiotic flow. This electricity did connect them.

He had not been with a woman for months. He missed it. He missed the feel of a woman. He missed the smell of one so close to him that he could pick up the different scents, from the perfume to the hint of perspiration. A woman could be, by smell alone, intoxicating. It was the only kind of intoxication he allowed himself.

As much as he missed the touch, the warmth, the hot breath, and the fiery passion, he knew what a relationship at work could mean. At best, conflict driven by passions that had nothing to do with the job. At its worst? Helping to bury a fellow officer with whom he had just slept with a few nights before. Life was about loss, like loss was fat insoluble, and when it had built up enough in his system, it was near fatal, the grief alone a killer.

He had taken risks in relationships. He'd taken some heavy hits. Now, here he was again, faced with a woman he found attractive, one who obviously found him attractive, ready to go where he had sworn too many times before he would not go again. Would he ever learn?

Before the night was out, he was sure he would have to decide if he would sleep with Jill or not.

He bought a bottle of wine before he went back to his room to shower, shave, and change clothes.

He arrived on time. On time was important. It had been drilled into him in the army and then again as a policeman. But more so, his mother had grilled it into him. Being too early or late, she had told him, was a comment on him. In neither case was it a good comment.

His father had his own slant to being on time. He said that some people thought you were anal if you were on time, but that was the excuse they used for being late. On time, he said, was the difference from getting to the fire at its start or at its end. His father had been a fireman who had died from complications from smoke inhalation when he had gone back into a burning house to search for a child.

His mother, so completely in love with and dedicated to his father, seemed to wither slowly after he died, until she joined him two years later. Both had died in their early 40s, one the result of a heroic effort and the other from heartbreak.

Jill seemed pleased that he was on time. Dinner was nearly ready. She had just enough time to put a slight chill on the wine he had purchased. He had been thoughtful enough to buy a wine that was better when it was drunk cool instead of cold.

The apartment was interesting, he thought. On the third floor of an architecturally uninspired building, she had done the best she could with it. The rooms were small, with very high ceilings. The windows were tall and narrow as well. She painted the walls in a cream color, and she used soft lighting to accent the slender slabs of walls and the windows with dark wood casings. She chose furniture that was much darker beige, and then she used throws and pillows with vibrant colors to accent it.

The apartment had a small kitchen with a tiny dining area attached, the living room, and a bedroom with a bath attached. In the bathroom, he discovered later, was a stacked washer and dryer. How to get his laundry done in Paris was still a mystery to him.

While she finished the dinner and set the table, he snooped. Her stereo was a good one. The television was new, and she had both a VCR and DVD player attached to it. The music was mostly soft rock by women vocalists. The DVDs and tapes leaned toward light, romantic comedy. Both the music and the movies were the kind that would entertain without demanding a lot intellectually. They were the kinds of things to which someone would turn in order to relax.

Dinner was French. She had learned well in her cooking classes. She served chestnut soup with white truffles, veal smothered in a mushroom sauce, and artichokes. Dessert was an almond cheesecake.

Dinner was served on nice china placed on a lace tablecloth. Lights were dimmed and candles lighted. She apologized for such a simple meal, but this was the best she could do in the time she had. He assured her the meal was excellent, and that any more would have been overdoing it.

They talked quietly but awkwardly. This was not work. This was something else. No matter how comfortable he might be with her at work, this was about a relationship outside of the workplace. They would have to go through a time-honored ritual of learning about each other. The chemistry between them seemed to work, but now another level of mutual compatibility needed to be probed. Yes, maybe they would enjoy going to bed with each other, but would they have anything to talk about in the morning? Would a sexual relationship bring an unwanted tension to the workplace? Would it even work? Perhaps the more they learned about each other, the less they would like each other.

He helped her clear the table and do the dishes. She seemed impressed, but he didn't think about it. He'd been a bachelor for a lot of years, living alone most of those. He could shop, he could cook, he could do the laundry, he could clean, and he could even sew if he had to. In the end it wasn't a big deal, and if a woman was impressed by it, he wondered what the men she knew didn't do, that such simple things could be so impressive.

After everything was clean and put away, they moved to the living room with their wine. He sat in the chair. She sat on the love seat and curled her feet under her, with her arm on the back so she could rest her head on her hand. When she was comfortable, she asked, "Are you as uneasy about this as I am?"

He liked honesty in a woman. He didn't see enough of it. "I don't think this qualifies as a date dinner, if that's what you mean. More like a wait-and-see dinner."

"A what?"

He twirled the stem of his wineglass and watched the light of the room play its way through the red wine. He took his time. He wasn't one to share too much of himself with a woman, and certainly nothing personal this early in a relationship. "It was something my mother said when I went out with a girl for the first time. She said it would be a wait-and-see date. Afterward, I'd just have to wait and see what came of it."

"She would have been a difficult woman for a girl to compete with."

"Not really," he said. "She stayed out of my relationships. That bit of wisdom was as much as I would get out of her, even if I had a second date and she got to meet the girl."

"I bet you had lots of second dates."

"Some," he said.

"Not all of them went to a second date?"

"Nope."

"Why not?"

"It didn't seem like a good use of my time," he said.

She laughed. "Will we have a second date?"

"Was this the first?" he asked.

She ran a finger around the rim of the glass and stared into the wine. In time, she said, "I think so."

"The dinner alone would warrant a second date. The fact that you have a washer and dryer might lead to a marriage proposal."

She didn't lift her eyes from her wineglass, but she did smile. "What would people think if they saw you bringing your clothes to my place?"

"I would think they would say, how French of them."

She lifted her eyes to his. "You're different," she said.

"Different? There's a word that can go in a lot of directions."

"Different from what I expected. Different from other men."

"What did you expect?"

"I wasn't sure. I guessed that the shooting had either hardened you, or it drove you out of police work. I expected someone either up-tight and defensive or terribly frail."

"I'm all of those things at the right moment of the night."

"Do you want to talk about it?"

"Boston's a very sophisticated place. Shoot someone and they line up the counselors and the therapists. They talk you to death for weeks on end, and then they declare you cured."

"Are your cured?"

"Moment by moment the boy dies, moment by moment I have a choice to make, and moment by moment I can't believe I made the wrong choice."

"How could you know it was the wrong choice?"

"The boy died."

"It could have been you."

She let her eyes drift back to the wineglass. "Where does that leave you? Hiding out from yourself in Paris?"

"I'm not hiding out. I'm starting over," he said. "I might stop dreaming about it someday, but I'll never forget I killed a kid. By moving my life in a new direction, I'm making sure I won't kill another kid."

"I don't see you in this job for the long haul. What will you do after this?"

"In some ways, this is part of the long haul. I started investigating the Assassin years ago. I'm still investigating him. I want to catch him."

"Do you see this as the thing that gives your life purpose and meaning?"

He could see his face in a mirror next to the front door. He shifted his head slightly, and his eyes disappeared into the shadows of the room. He wondered what she would do when she could no longer read the expression on his face. "I see it as unfinished business," he said. "What gives your life purpose and meaning?"

She shifted on the sofa to get a better view of his face, but his eyes remained in the shadows. "Some days I wake up thinking I want to move up in the ranks of the foreign service and eventually become a powerful figure in our government. Some days I wake up and want to cry because I'm not married, and I don't have children, and I'm so far away from my family."

"But you don't cry because you have the strength not to. In the end you pride yourself in getting through another day with your dignity intact. You go to bed at night feeling a little bit guilty because you like this too much, and you don't think you should because you don't have a husband, and children, and a place in your hometown. More than anything, you are afraid that if you break down and conform, you'll live a life of boredom."

She eyed him for a moment and then replied to his last sentence. "Let me assure you that this job has its share of boredom."

"Help me find the Assassin. I think he lives in Paris. I just don't know how to find him."

"How can you be so sure he lives in Paris?"

"I feel it," he said.

Finally she lowered her feet to the floor and moved so she could see his eyes again. "I don't understand you at all," she said.

"I don't know if anyone can understand anyone else."

She placed her glass on the coffee table and then she stepped over to him and took his glass to set it down beside hers. Then she took his hand and pulled him to his feet and led him to the front door. "I want you to kiss me goodnight as if I were the most desirable woman on earth. And then I want you to go home before I have another glass of wine and make a decision that might ruin this evening for both of us."

He took her in his arms and kissed her. The kiss started slowly and then gained a life of its own until their two bodies were straining against each other. When the kiss finally ended, and he could finally find his voice, he said, "I don't know if I understand you."

"Go to bed tonight and dream about me instead of that boy in the alley."

The next morning, after he had crawled out of his bed and finished half of his morning routine, the thought struck him. He had dreamed about her. And, for the first time since it had happened, he had not dreamed about the boy he had shot.

ELEVEN

She beat him to work. Jill was sitting at her desk listening to messages on her voice mail and taking notes as she did. When he walked in, she glanced up and smiled. He smiled back.

He checked his voice mail. He had one message from Gerard, who said he could see them at ten, and he had a second one from a James Smith at Interpol. He was asked to return the call.

They hung up their phones at the same time. Jill was the first to speak. "If a girl could get pregnant from a kiss," she said, "then I know I'm pregnant."

He liked that about her, too. She wasn't afraid to confront the uncomfortable. "I dreamed about you last night," he said.

"Not about the boy?"

"Not about the boy."

"And what did you dream about me?"

He opened his notebook and scanned through it, to see if he had run across the name James Smith before. He hadn't. He took enough time to make the silence between them awkward, and then he said, "We'll have to know each other better for me to tell you. Do you know who James Smith is at Interpol?"

"Very good. First you dodge the question, and then you redirect the conversation. It must have been a hell of a dream." When she saw that he wasn't going to respond, she said, "I don't know who he is."

He walked into the conference room and poured himself a cup of coffee, and then he came back to his desk. As he sat, he asked, "Any pressing business?"

"Another lost passport. Some stolen traveler's checks. An accident in a rental car. The embassy has advised everyone involved, and have directed the folks to us if they have any further questions. We may or may not hear from them. Other than that, we're pretty free for the day. I already told the Legat Office to direct calls to our cell phones."

"Gerard says he will see us at ten."

"Good. Let me tidy up a few things on my desk, and then we can walk to the police headquarters, and maybe have a cup of coffee along the way."

While she did that, Grant returned the call to James Smith at Interpol. He was surprised to find that James Smith, with such a good American name, was actually British. He was even more surprised to find that Smith was the Interpol expert on the Assassin, and he wanted to talk to Grant, the American expert on the Assassin.

Over the phone, Smith said, "When I saw your name on a report that crossed my desk about the Sutherby/Saldano hits, I couldn't believe my bloody good fortune. I remember well the work you did on the case in Boston."

"I appreciate that," Grant said. "I was planning to call you—or call the person who was the Interpol expert on the Assassin. This is definitely a bad guy who needs catching."

Smith chuckled. "That's rather mild. I couldn't repeat what we've said about him, even on a secure telephone line. I called because I had some questions for you."

"Go ahead."

"You have no doubt in your mind that it is the work of the Assassin? This couldn't be what you Yanks call a copycat or a protégé? The Assassin has been out of circulation for some time. I was surprised to see him reappear."

"Pop, pop, pop—right locations, right sequence," Grant said. "The suspected shooter was seen, but he wasn't seen. He was a man with his head turned, a man with a hat pulled low over his eyes, a man in the shadows, a man who defied description. On the video from the store in Boston, he appeared on camera for less than three seconds. His head was turned away and down. He was wearing a hat. He was hunched over in an overcoat too large for him. From the video we couldn't even tell what race he was, what nationality, what height, what weight. The man the witnesses caught sight of in the club before the two were killed defied description. In the shadows, wearing a hat pulled low over his eyes, head turned away when they looked in his direction. I can't imagine it being anyone but the Assassin."

"I tend to agree. The only thing that bothers me is his long period of inactivity."

"Why do you think he was inactive for so long?"

"The hit on a politician in a crowded grocery store in broad daylight might look to someone on the outside as foolhardy. I thought it was brilliant. When was the last time you felt in danger in a grocery store?"

"Right, right. So you think the people who hired him thought he might be over the hill for a hit man?"

"I think that's a possibility."

"Then why go back to the bugger?"

"Expedience."

"I have absolutely nothing to back this up, but I think the Assassin lives in Paris or close by. I think the hit was a hurried decision, and I think the Assassin was the closest hit man around to take care of it."

"Again, expedience. What makes you think he lives in Paris?"

If he were talking to another cop, one he had worked with before and had trusted, he could simply answer that he had a hunch. Cops understood hunches. They came from some deep reservoir of experience, so many and over such a long time, that the source had long ago disappeared into the subconscious. A cop trusted his hunches. Hunches sometimes solved crimes. Hunches sometimes saved the cop's life. "I don't have any evidence, of course," Grant replied with caution. "When you track his thirty hits, and then you throw in maybe another dozen we suspect but can't confirm because folks in those countries don't share information the way we do, and then you notice one major country left out of the loop, it makes you wonder why. Every country that touches France, including Monaco, has at least one hit in it by the Assassin."

"Run that number up to fifty. Since the Assassin has been inactive, I've had nothing better to do than go back and research other hits. I think I can lay fifty on the Assassin's doorstep. And, up until a few days ago, none had taken place in France."

"You're in France, I'm in France, and the Assassin is probably in France, yet we're no closer to catching him than before. What is the unraveled thread that will lead us back to the cloak thrown over the Assassin that seems to make him invisible?"

Jill, still sitting at her desk and typing in a memo to herself on her computer's calendar, said, without glancing up, "Hats."

"Who was that?" Smith asked.

"That was my associate, Jill St. Claire. She just said 'hats.'"

"You used the word 'hats' three times in one short discussion," Jill said. "Maybe he always wears the same hat. Maybe you can trace him by his hat."

Grant stared at her. She sat, quietly absorbed in her typing, saying "Damn" when she had to back space to make a correction, without realizing for a moment her own brilliance.

"She wondered if he might wear the same hat in all the hits," he said, desperately fighting down a spike of excitement. Could something so simple be the first break in the case? Then the feeling of excitement disappeared. The Assassin was too smart to wear the same hat each time.

"Christ," Smith said. "It would take a woman to focus on how the bloody man was dressed. I never thought about the hat. I would think the Assassin too smart to wear the same hat twice."

"Yeah," Grant said. "I can't see him wearing it again and again."

Again without looking up, Jill said, "It doesn't matter if he wore it once or fifty times. You've got a picture of him with a hat on his head. If he's French, and if he bought the hat here, maybe you can trace it."

The sense of excitement came back. "Jill said—"

"I heard her. The woman's brilliant. Don't let her get away. The first thing I'm going to do is to get one of our artists to make a drawing from the photo we have, and then I'm going to fax it to each place where a hit was carried out. Then I'm going to ask the police to check with their witnesses and see if they recognize the hat. If the old chap wore it more than once, then chances are good he bought it where he lived and carried it back and forth with him."

"Let me know as soon as you find out."

"I will," Smith said. "And thank you."

After he hung up the phone, Grant said to Jill, "He said you were brilliant and not to lose you."

She was still struggling to get the memo typed correctly. She made a face at the computer screen, and then she said,

"The obtuse always think the less obtuse are brilliant. I can't type worth a damn today. Let's go get some coffee."

After they had closed up the office and were walking toward a table outside of the restaurant at la place St-Michel, Grant asked, "What do you think the chances are of the hat leading to anything?"

"Ten thousand to one," she said, "but nothing leading to something has much higher odds."

"How'd you get to be so smart?"

"My mother called it smart; my father called it being a smartass."

They sat down and ordered coffee. Despite Grant's limited knowledge of the language, he could at least do that. But the waiter still gave him a smirking grin, knowing he was an American. "Do you really think the odds are that bad?"

"Not if he likes expensive hats, and he buys them in Paris."

"Why is it now starting to sound too easy?" he asked.

"The difference between too hard and too easy is finding the answer."

He wanted to laugh at her. He even wanted to make fun of her. She sounded like some wizened old grandmother. On the other hand, these things seemed to roll off her tongue without a substantial thought behind them. Could it be that she was an anomaly? Was she a woman who was brilliant only when she didn't think about something?

"Quit trying to figure me out," she said. "I'm odd, I know. I came this way out of the box. I'm used to it now. Dale says I drive him nuts." She put her chin on her hands and smiled sweetly at him.

"I'm impressed," he said.

"Whadja think? They hired me for my good looks and charm?"

"I thought it might be for your cooking."

She reached out and patted the back of one of his hands. "You I like. On the other hand, don't get that male chauvinistic idea that you're the only one who thinks about things and we women just feel them. Ever since Saldano and Sutherby got killed, I've been doing a lot of research and giving it a lot of thought. You're not the only one who knows how to use a computer and to access Interpol. By the way, your report on the Assassin was exceptional, by far the most intelligent of any written about him."

"Are you going to keep surprising me all at once, or are you going to mete it out over time?"

"By the time I'm done, you're going to like me a lot."

"I don't doubt it for a minute," he said, as he put his chin in his hands and stared back into her eyes.

Inside la Police Criminelle was exactly as he imagined it to be. The building was full of long, narrow, high-ceilinged hallways, and the space had been chopped up into small offices with the same high ceilings. Inspector Gerard's office fitted his status. His office overlooked the Seine. The two of them were led into his office by a receptionist/secretary who apparently served several inspectors. She spoke excellent English, Grant noted.

The office was small, but the walls were lined with bookshelves that went to the ceiling, and the shelves were filled with both books and personal items of the inspector's. These included several framed degrees and certificates, pictures of his family, and photos of himself taken with various officials. The inspector himself greeted them with his coat off, his tie loose around his neck, and his sleeves rolled up. He invited them to sit in the only other two chairs in the room besides the one behind his desk.

When they were all comfortable, the inspector said, "I wish I could give you some more information about the murders, but we still don't know much. As I said before, forensics has yet to come up with anything useful. The rain that night did not help, and the murderer has a history of not leaving much behind in the way of clues."

"Are you any closer to finding out which of the two was the intended target?" Grant asked. He noticed that the inspector, even though he spoke English quite well, needed to sort words to make sure he understood what was being asked of him. He knew that was true of the academic linguists. They could speak a language with fluency, but they had a struggle understanding when it was spoken to them. Grant guessed that it was because they didn't get enough practice conversing with native speakers.

Gerard said, "*Non*. From what we have learned so far, neither of them has anything in their pasts that would warrant a professional hit."

"It doesn't help," Jill added, "that each has parents or grandparents who could have been the reason for either one of them being killed."

Gerard was quicker to respond this time, Grant noticed. Like many people and foreign languages, he seemed to have an easier time understanding a female voice than a male voice. "*Oui*," he said. "On one side, it could have been political. On the other side, it could have had something to do with money. All of the relatives involved insist that it has nothing to do with them."

Gerard had had better luck than he had, Grant thought. Tiffany's parents were not exactly a wealth of information. "You have talked with Walter Sutherlin then?" he asked.

Gerard shrugged apologetically. "Someone within our government talked to a representative of his. My government feels that this is one of those delicate situations with both victims that should be handled diplomatically. As you must know from your experience, few people see the police as being diplomatic."

"I will see if I can talk to the man."

Jill added quickly to Gerard, "That is, of course, if the State Department thinks it's a good idea."

He nodded his head in her direction and smiled. He'd just been overruled. "Of course," he said, keeping most of the sarcasm out of his voice. "Have you any theories about motive?" he asked.

Gerard moved from his desk to the window and glanced out the window at the River Seine across the street. "Hatred, jealousy, revenge, money: we are exploring each one. Perhaps one of the two had a rich ex-lover. Maybe one of them made someone very angry. We are finding out as much as we can about the two. I would be glad to share whatever we find out with you, as long as you, naturally, will share what you find out."

"That's a given," Jill said.

Gerard didn't appear to understand that, Grant thought. He added, "Of course we will."

"I understand that you are working with James Smith," he said to Grant.

News travels fast, Grant noted. In the future he would assume that to be the case. "Yes."

Gerard turned back to the two of them. "James knows more about the Assassin than anyone except maybe the Assassin himself. He's also dedicated years to not finding the man. Let me caution you that James, now on a religious mission when it comes to the Assassin, tends to play his cards close to his vest—yes, I think that is the expression."

"You mean he doesn't share," Jill said.

"Yes," Gerard said, "but he is always polite about it."

Jill burst out laughing and Gerard looked confused. "I'm sorry," she said. "The way you put that was funny."

"What do you know," he said. "In my language I'm not

known for my sense of humor, but in yours I might become a standout comedian."

Close enough, Grant thought. If not a stand-up comedian, at least a stand-up police officer. And then, for absolutely no good reason at all, he suddenly felt confident that he and Gerard would capture the Assassin, and that James Smith would never forgive them for it.

TWELVE

He paused at the doors. Perhaps he was getting too old for this, he thought. He had almost walked without his hat into the elevator that led from his apartment. He turned back to the ornate stand near the elevator doors, an antique piece that was hand-carved from oak. It had a small bench seat that opened to storage. On each side were coat trees, and around the arched curve that outlined the mirror that filled its high back were a series of pegs for hats. The hat he wanted was not hanging around the top of the mirror. It was in the storage box under the seat. This was a special hat, and he did not want it seen by anyone who knew him.

He removed the hat and then carried it in his hand under a light raincoat draped over his arm so the hat was hidden beneath it. He would not put it on until long after he had passed the concierge and had walked several blocks from his building. This was his hunting hat. This was the hat that had given him such good luck over the years.

What made the hat special was the wide brim that folded down so naturally in the front. With the rim down over his eyes, his dark glasses on, and his raincoat turned up at the collar, almost nothing of his features could be seen. The raincoat was special, too, because it was oversized. It hung on him in such a way that little could be made of his physical features, working in much the same way as a granny dress did for a woman.

The coat had another special feature. He had removed the lining of the right pocket so that he could reach under the coat and pull the silenced automatic from his sports coat pocket. For this special occasion, he had chosen a cheap .22 automatic with a silencer he had fashioned himself. The silencer was much rounder and shorter than most, but this allowed him to fit the small weapon with the silencer attached into his pocket. It wasn't a pretty combination, but he had tested it, and it worked. Besides, within a half hour the gun would be in the river.

He wasn't a foolish man. In the last two years resentment had grown in him when he realized that the people who hired him stopped calling. They apparently saw the murder of the woman in the grocery store in America as a foolhardy hit, not a cunningly clever assassination. They seemed to overlook the fact that he had killed the woman as planned and he had gotten away with it, clean. The American press tended to get hysterical for short spurts when something sensational came along, but they got over it rather quickly. The people who hired him took all of this more seriously than he did. They stopped calling.

Long ago he had learned about the Paris company that often hired him, and he had learned the names of each member without these men suspecting. He learned what he could about each of them, and had cautiously tracked each of them so he knew where they lived, their habits, and their weaknesses. He never took advantage of the knowledge, but tracking a prey was in his nature because this is what would ultimately lead to a successful kill.

He learned that most of the people he killed for them were intended to be a statement to someone else. Money was at the heart of most such murders, and these killings were no different. His clients did not want him to kill the source of the money, but someone close enough to the source to get a message across. He could only guess what the message might be, because he was given only the information they thought he needed to make the kill. More than likely the message was "pay up." In some cases the message might be "back off." As best he could tell from what he knew, the latest kill carried a message of "don't."

Now it was his turn to send a message. Neither "back off" nor "pay up" applied. "Don't" did, though. Don't mess with him. Don't turn your back on him. Don't underestimate him. He was sure they would get the message.

He had chosen to make his statement with the death of Augustus de Bienne. He chose this man for a reason. Like his last target, the man was only on the peripheral. His death would serve only one purpose, and that was to send a message. de Bienne was sort of a salesman in this unusual corporation and not an executive—if he needed to send another message, he would eliminate an executive the next time. This man was careless. He never for a moment thought of himself as a potential target. Finally, he did not like the man's name. Augustus was simply too pretentious a name for a man who was basically a common crook.

And he was a common crook with common taste. When the weather was nice, de Bienne would go to the Latin Quarter for lunch. He would stop and order a ham and cheese crêpe and a little something to drink from a street vendor on la Rue de St. Severin, and then stop at a shop to pick up an assortment of chocolates. He would carry these to the grounds of the Church de St. Severin, and there, sitting on a bench, he would slowly eat, sharing his meals with the birds that would gather at his feet or hover near his hands.

He made no attempt to follow de Bienne from his office building. Instead he walked to the Church de St. Severin. He, too, sat on a bench, but one far from de Bienne's usual perch. Ten minutes later the salesman appeared and took up his normal position.

He killed the man with calculated efficiency with a half a dozen people within twenty feet of them. He came up to de Bienne's bench from behind. With his left hand he patted de Bienne on the shoulder, calling out his name. His right hand came out of his pocket with the gun in it; he put the weapon at the base of the salesman's skull.

He continued to move around to the front of de Bienne. The other man glanced up when he heard his name, but his eyes failed to note recognition. The first bullet smashed into the back of de Bienne's head, and his expression shifted to one of distress while his body struggled for control that was suddenly interrupted. The gun moved as he moved, so that when he was around in front of de Bienne his body and his baggy raincoat blocked the view of anyone who might have noticed them. He fired a second time to the temple. De Bienne's body slumped but he had already grabbed the man's right arm to keep him from toppling over.

He leaned over the man now, as if the two were sharing a quiet and intimate conversation. de Bienne's mouth had gone slack so it was easy to slip the silencer into it to finish the job. He continued to lean over the body as if still in conversation with de Bienne. This gave him time to slip the gun back in his pocket, to prop the body up on the park bench, and to pick up the food that had fallen from de Bienne's hand.

When he stepped back to say his goodbyes, he left behind an interesting tableau. de Bienne sat slumped on the bench with his chin on his chest, one hand holding a crêpe in his lap and the other wrapped around his drink that rested on the bench next to him. His eyes were open and seemed to stare down at the birds that now began to gather around him, ready to collect a free meal. From a distance he looked like a man in contemplation. Someone would have to come to him from behind to notice the blood on the back of his head. The hair around his ear and his sideburn hid the small trickle of blood that came from the second head wound.

He smiled and waved, saying *"Au revoir"* as he left, circling back around the bench and leaving the way from which he had come.

Two of the six who were nearby at the time of the murder would give a description of the shooter, but in both cases they would not come forward until the next day. None of the six had been aware that a man had been killed close to them. In fact, it wouldn't be for another half an hour before two young lovers, walking hand in hand along the path, would discover the dead man. Their attention was tugged away from each other by the strange sight of a man sitting on a park bench with dozens of birds fighting over the food in his lap.

None of the witnesses who saw the man approach the bench could describe his physical features. All admitted that they had not paid that much attention to the sight of two men, apparently friends, meeting on a bench in Paris, a scene carried out a thousand times a day. No one saw a gun, heard a shot, or noticed any indication the man on the bench had been murdered. No one could say for sure that they remembered the second man leaving. Nothing they had noticed suggested anything out of the ordinary, and all had gone back to what they were doing within seconds of seeing the killer approach the bench.

By the time the man returned to his building, he was quite pleased with himself. The gun had slipped into the River Seine unnoticed. While walking along the quay, he paused for a moment, as if to get a closer look at a houseboat tied up to the walkway, and it was then that he let the gun slip from under his raincoat and into the water.

And he also was quite pleased with himself because he had been able to leave his unmistakable signature. The message would get across clearly.

The next day, when Grant finally got to see a copy of the French crime report on the shooting sent to him by Gerard and translated by Jill, he called the inspector before he had finished reading it. He had three questions for the inspector: Who was Augustus de Bienne? Could the witnesses describe the hat the killer wore? What made the witnesses think the two men were friends?

On the other end of the phone line, Gerard smiled when he heard the questions. The first two he had asked already. The third one, though, he had not thought to ask. If the Assassin behaved like a friend, did that mean the two knew each other? And, of course, he had learned from the witnesses that the Assassin appeared to be a Frenchman through his dress and mannerisms, a fact supporting Grant's theory that the man lived in France.

THIRTEEN

Grant woke up early, before the sun. He showered, shaved, and dressed, and then he walked the short distance to the Cathédrale de Notre Dame. He kneeled in a pew in the back, away from the altar where a priest prepared for an early Mass, and he said prayers for the dead. Before he left, he lit a candle for the boy he had shot, and he lit two more for Tiffany and Escobar, and a fourth for de Bienne.

By the time he left the church, the sun had risen but it was obscured by thick clouds, leaving the morning gray and heavy with dew. The odors from the night hung thick in the air: the smell of urine from the stairs to the river, the odd earthy and fishy smell of the muddy waters of the Seine between its rock banks, the hint of metal in the smell of wet stone. He walked until he picked up the baked and yeasty aroma of fresh bread. In a small café he bought a hot petit pain and a large, cup of steaming coffee, unusual because it was not so close to the texture of molasses that the French seemed to like so much. He walked to the Place St. Andre des Arts and sat on a step while he ate the hot bread and washed it down with the coffee. He still felt hungry.

He was building up energy. He was preparing for the hunt. The Assassin was somewhere nearby, and he had made a fatal error. He had killed again, not far from where he had killed before, and he had left his signature to send a signal to someone. He had not walked away from his last hit as he should have, a precaution that had worked so well for him before when he would not show up again until months later in some other part of the world.

Somewhere in all of that was a clue. Sift through it and the thread would rise to the surface that would lead Grant to the killer. He was sure of it. He now had to practice a stoic patience because he was not playing this game on his own field. He was frustrated because Gerard had not invited him to the scene of the crime. He wasn't being cut out of the loop, he knew, because Gerard had contacted Interpol as soon as he knew the hit was the work of the Assassin, and he had filed a preliminary report about the crime scene. By doing this, he made the information available to Grant.

Protocol. The victim had been a Frenchman. To call in the Americans was out of the question. A diplomatic request to share information would take time. When all had been done correctly, Gerard would call Grant and invite him to visit again.

Grant had learned that the victim was an agent for a brokerage firm that dealt in works of art. Although he wanted to let his mind run wild, making connections with the other victims, he did not. He did not need fantastic ideas; he needed information. He had to wait even though he was not very good at waiting.

He knew that the sooner an investigation began the better the chances that it would lead to a solution. Memories faded quickly or they were influenced by what the witnesses read in the newspaper or saw in the news. Often the insignificant could provide a clue. In one case the solution came from the fact that the criminal wore his wedding ring upside down. These were the little things that faded first from memory.

In the long run, big chunks were forgotten. Witnesses moved away. Interest began to fade as other crime files stacked up on the ones below them. Grant wanted to talk to the people who had been in the park. He wanted to interview the shopkeepers in the area who might have seen the killer on the way to commit the crime. He wanted to fan out from the sight of the killing and see if he could find anyone who saw the man walk away.

From the accounts that Grant had read so far, the man seemed to leave in a direction away from a metro station. He might have parked on the street, but he had walked in the direction of the Sorbonne, where parking was at a premium. He wasn't likely to have found a space, and if he had, some parking was by permit only. Perhaps his car had been ticketed. Better yet, maybe he had continued walking. If that were the case, they might be able to pinpoint the area of the city from which he came.

Why was that important? One part of the city specialized in hotels. Another specialized in apartments. Some areas had permanent residences. Maybe, just maybe, the Assassin walked to work. If he could just be included in the investigation—

Two shapely legs stopped in front of him. He recognized them as Jill's. He smiled to himself and said, without looking up, "Good morning, Jill."

"What's it mean when a co-worker can recognize you by your legs?" she asked.

"It means you've got nice legs," he said.

She sat down beside him. "This time I'll accept that as a compliment. Next time I'll nail your butt to the wall for sexual harassment."

"Does that mean you've been looking at my butt?"

She tilted her head sideways and briefly rested it on his shoulder. "Let's not go there," she said.

"Is that a form of taking the fifth?" he teased.

"I think we've both checked each other out and liked what we saw. Right now I suspect you weren't sitting here thinking about my legs. I bet you were trying to figure out how you could worm your way into the police's investigation into this latest murder."

"A mind reader all the way."

"Dale called me at home before I left for work. He had a very clear message for both of us—stay out, stay out, stay out. Even if we get an invitation from the French to participate in this investigation in any way, shape, or form—his cliché—we are not to do a thing without permission from the Legal Attaché himself."

"Is that Dale's normal protocol paranoia, or is that the word from the top?"

"He got a phone call before I got a phone call."

Grant nodded. He hadn't expected anything less. "Is it lost passports, missing travelers checks, or stolen cars today?"

"I thought we might see if we could find a connection between our two murders and the most recent one."

"Isn't that in violation of Dale's orders?"

"Dale didn't say we couldn't continue our investigation into the murder of an American."

He stood up and then reached down to take one of Jill's hands to help her up. "I like the way you think," he said. "I like the way you cook, too."

"No telling what else you will learn to like about me," she said.

"No telling," he said, as they walked away together. Only after they had taken a few steps did he realize he still held her hand. He gave it a squeeze and then let go of it. He wouldn't want anyone to think the troops were fraternizing.

When they got to the office and settled in, Jill said to him, "I'll see what I can find out about the man who was murdered. You see what you can find out about the company he worked for."

Jill, with her mastery of French, first went to the phone. Grant went to the Internet. It took both of them only a short time before they realized the task wasn't going to be as easy as they had thought. Neither the man nor his company seemed to want people to know much about them.

Grant spent the rest of the day on his computer, interrupted twice by phone calls from Herbert Ingrahm, the Assistant Legal Attaché. One call was a request to confirm hotel stays and dates for an American suspected of illegally selling computer equipment to Russian agents. The second call involved a second American who was thought to be, in a minor way, a French connection for importing drugs into the United States. He was believed to be using his animal transport service as a means of shipping drugs.

Jill made the phone calls to confirm the hotel stays. Grant checked out the transport service on the Internet. The man's company arranged everything from shipping zoo animals to pets and racehorses from the continent to America. He chartered transport planes, and then he arranged for his own handlers and flight crews to make the deliveries. The chance to smuggle drugs in such an operation would be more than tempting.

The Legat Office wanted dates of flights and itineraries. Grant was told that the two of them might have to do some footwork later on, including seeking out and interviewing flight crewmembers and animal handlers who lived in France, but only those who were Americans. The French police and Interpol would be contacting any non-Americans. This seemed like an incredibly inefficient way of doing business, but Jill reassured him that both of these organizations were very good at what they did and cooperation between them often made these types of investigations seamless. Grant, still smarting from being left out of the last murder, would have to be convinced.

By the end of the day, he'd found time to work on the triple murder case and what he'd learned about Euro-Arts, the company for which the Assassin's latest victim worked. He learned that Euro-Arts was a very low-profile organization, très exclusif, so much so that he found out only a little about it. The company did not own a store that he could locate, did not have a showroom he knew of, nor did it run an Internet site. It had a phone number. When he tried the number, Grant got a recording asking him to leave his name, his number, and a reference.

Reference? This set off little alarm bells in the back of Grant's mind. This was a ploy used by escort services in Boston to keep the cops at bay. In the case of Euro-Arts, once a contact was made, a representative, a salesperson, so to speak, such as Augustus de Bienne, would fly any-where in the world for a face-to-face meeting.

Grant only had a vague idea of what transpired between the company and the clients, mainly because he could find no substantial piece of information about Euro-Arts. A museum acknowledged Euro-Arts' help in obtaining a Picasso sketch. Interpol had a file nearly empty, with a standing request for information about the company from any police agency in the world. A highbrow art magazine criticized Euro-Arts for corrupting the exclusiveness of world masterpieces.

As Grant understood it, Euro-Arts had three divisions. One offered the works of talented and expensive new art-ists. The second division arranged private sales of known works of arts, providing authentication of the work and handling the financial transactions. The third division was the one that was controversial: Euro-Arts commissioned some of these fine new artists to create replications of masterpieces. These were not reproductions, but in essence commissioned and apparently legal forgeries. From what he had read, Grant was convinced that Euro-Arts obtained, when it needed to, permission to paint the copy, and the company advertised these as copies. What inspired people to pay apparently substantial prices for these copies was that they were as good as a superior forgery.

Grant would have to know more about the company than he did now to find a connection between it and the Assassin. He would also have to do more research to see if he could find a connection between Euro-Arts and Walter Sutherlin.

His search for information on Euro-Arts had led him in strange directions on the Internet. One of them was to a website sponsored by both the FBI and Interpol. From it, Grant learned that an estimated $3 billion in stolen artwork was unaccounted for around the world. This represented more than 100,000 works of arts that had been stolen and then had simply disappeared. The list included 121 works by Rembrandt, 250 by Chagall, 180 by Dali, 115 by Renoir, and 350 by Picasso.

The paintings and other works of art were stolen in a variety of ways, from sophisticated break-ins to smash-and-snatch daylight thefts. Although the best of museums had extensive security systems, thousands of smaller museums around the world could not afford such luxuries, especially when only one or two pieces they had held any astronomical value. For a sophisticated, dedicated thief, stealing these was akin to shoplifting a candy bar, Grant thought.

He sat back in his chair, put his hands behind his head and his feet on his desk, and contemplated the space outside the left window in the office. Jill glanced at him once and smiled. She knew he was thinking, and it was best not to disturb the process. She liked the notion that he was a thinker, and that he liked to look at a problem from a lot of different ways. Dale often dead-ended too easily and passed skimpy data on to the Legat Office. Grant didn't impress her as someone who would give up easily at all.

His eyes came back into focus, and he turned to Jill and asked, "Where would you look for a hundred thousand pieces of stolen art, all of which has gone missing in the last few decades?"

"Ideally, among the things I've purchased in a thrift shop."

"I wouldn't hold my breath on that one."

"Not all art thieves are very adept at what they do. I suspect that some of that artwork was destroyed in the attempt to steal it. I would guess, too, that hot art might not be that easy to unload. Again, a thief stuck with a painting he can't sell and one that could send him to prison might decide to destroy it in time. Other pieces might be stored in an attic or a storage facility, waiting for the heat to die down so they can be sold with less risk involved. I'm sure other pieces have ended up in the hands of private collectors."

"Why would a private collector want to have a piece of art he dare not share with anyone?"

"I don't know that I can answer that," she said. "Only a handful of original Ferrari GTOs exist. Over the last decade or so, these have changed hands on the market for anywhere from three million to eleven million dollars. Ferrari has gone to court to stop anyone from making a copy of his car. The only way to own one is to buy a model of it or have the funds for the real thing."

"I admire your knowledge about cars. But the point ...?"

"For your information, we once worked with an American who bought a GTO to help insure that it was shipped back to the U.S. safely."

"Is that one of our jobs, too?"

"He was a friend of a friend in a high place."

"I see," he said. "No misuse of power there."

She laughed. "We work for a democratic—political—system. Need I say more?"

"You haven't answered my question."

"Actually, before that nasty little interruption, I was about to answer your question. There's only one in the world and you want it. Unfortunately it's not for sale. You want it. You've got lots of money. You make it known you will pay anything to get it. Gosh, one day the painting is stolen, the next it's offered to you for sale. You got it. Do you really care how you got it? Do you really care if you have to hide it away? You have the satisfaction of knowing you have something that no one else has."

"I always thought it was the other way around. You got satisfaction from flaunting what no one else has."

"You obviously don't have a lot of money."

"You mean, 'The rich are very different from you and me?'" he asked.

"Fitzgerald?"

"Right."

"Hemingway said 'Yeah, they have more money.'"

"I think that means we're not going to be able to answer that question."

"I think that means for every person who buys a stolen work of art, you might find a different reason."

"One hundred thousand of them?"

"I wouldn't be surprised," she said. "All that heavy thinking has made me hungry. Why don't you buy me dinner?"

"It's too early for dinner," he said. "Fashionably, far too early."

"Then let's go be tourists until it's fashionable to eat. The Louvre is just across the river from here. Maybe admiring masterpieces will help answer the question for us."

He hadn't been to the Louvre yet. He had been told that the museum needed to be taken in over time, a room or two of artwork each visit or he would be overwhelmed by it. Today would be a good day to get that first sample of art. "I'll buy dinner if you buy the tickets to the Louvre," he said.

"Wonderful," she said, reaching into her desk drawer. "Oh, by the way, I forgot to tell you. The embassy provides us with free passes to the art museums in Paris. One of our fringe benefits." She held up two passes. "One of these is yours."

FOURTEEN

They toured Napoleon's apartment in the Louvre. They spent an hour, taking time to stand and stare into each of the rooms, Grant imagined that Napoleon himself might wander through. Jill convinced him that this was all that they should try to see on this visit, despite Grant's eagerness to continue exploring. Another time they might have a Mona Lisa visit and then a Venus de Milo visit, taking in the other works of art in each area. As she said, "One of the advantages of being here is you do not have to try to take in the Louvre in a day—a disaster, I assure you. You can take a year or two to appreciate it all."

Grant, however, didn't think he would be wandering in and out of the Louvre over the next two years. The Musée d'Orsay might be a different case though. This former train station had been converted into one of the finest museums in Europe and housed a spectacular collection of art from 1848 to 1914. Van Gogh, Manet, Monet, Degas, Renoir: they were all in this museum. Grant's taste in art leaned toward the Impressionists.

After a dinner of snails with garlic butter and sole meunière, the two had an awkward moment. Attracted to each other, both were being tugged toward a more intimate relationship. Both were professionals, though, and it was Grant who put it into words after dinner. "As much as I don't want to," he said, "I need to say goodnight to you here. I don't think another trip to your apartment would be wise right now."

Jill was not the least offended. During dinner, she had been struggling with what she would say to him that would send him home alone but not drive him away. She was glad when he brought it up first. "You're good company outside of the workplace," she said. "I want more of it. I'm going to need to feel more comfortable about the two of us before I'll feel good about more than just company."

He held her for a long time before kissing her goodnight. He left her at the Metro stop that would lead her home, and then he walked back to his room feeling content. In his life he'd had more women as friends than men. Sexual attraction could be a problem, but women didn't feel the need to compete with him as so many men he knew did. He would take Jill as a friend first. If that was all that came of it, then he was still ahead. He had a friend.

He got to the office first in the morning. He was on the phone after he had started the coffee. He placed a call to the States, requesting a return call from Walter Sutherlin. He placed a call to Gerard. He then placed a third call to Euro-Arts and left a message to call back. As a reference he replied that he was investigating a murder.

He expected a return call from Gerard. The call to Sutherlin, he was sure, would be answered through the embassy. He wouldn't be surprised if he got a message from the Legal Attaché himself, telling Grant to back off. He did not expect to hear from Euro-Arts at all.

Jill walked in as he hung up the phone for the last time. Today she was wearing a pair of gray slacks that complimented her lovely shape and a pale blue blouse with two buttons undone at the top. Her hair was pulled back in a ponytail and sunglasses rested on top of her head. The final piece to the ensemble was a dark gray, leather purse that hung over her left shoulder on a long strap. The purse rode on her left hip, and she had her hand draped over its flap.

"You look very cosmopolitan this morning," he said.

"I try to dress appropriately for the cosmos," she said.

"Exceptional job," he said.

She walked to his desk and leaned over the top slightly to look down into his lap. "Those are not blue jeans are they?"

"I believe they are."

"If Dale comes back today, he'll have a stroke. We do not wear blue jeans to work."

"Are you going to send me home and make me change?" he asked, trying his best to look contrite.

"No, I'm going to let you wear the jeans, and then I'm going to hope that Dale shows up."

"So you want him to have a stroke?"

"No, I want him to be the bad guy who sends you home to change."

He smiled to himself. He wasn't about to go back and change. He dressed as he felt, and today he felt like jeans. They could get used to it, or they could sputter and fume. The worst either one of them could do was to get him fired, and he knew that would take some doing, especially over a pair of jeans. He put the jeans behind him, opened a file, and began to review everything they knew about the murders. He wanted the facts fresh in his mind when Gerard called.

He was to be surprised twice that day. The first surprise came at ten in the morning when his phone rang. He answered it as he had been told to do, "U.S. Embassy, Legal Attaché Services. Grant Reynolds speaking."

After a long pause, as if someone was considering

whether or not they had the wrong number, a female voice said, "One moment, please." Grant listened to a moment of dead silence, the kind that came with a call being transferred, and then he heard a new voice, a male this time. "Grant Reynolds?"

"Yes it is," Grant said.

"U.S. Embassy Legal Attaché Services ... what exactly is that?"

The voice was definitely American, Grant realized as he listened. He would put the man's age somewhere in the thirties or forties. Although he hadn't said enough to tell for sure, Grant would bet that the man was college educated. "We help the embassy gather information about crimes committed against Americans in foreign countries. This particular branch, of course, deals with Americans in France."

"Then I have no idea why you would want to talk to me."

For a moment Grant thought the line would go dead, but the man waited silently on the other end. Grant made a guess. "Are you from Euro-Arts?"

The pause continued. Finally the voice said, "Yes. I'm Kyle Hosteller. I'm a representative of the company. Why do you want to talk to us?"

When he was a cop investigating a murder, he found that vinegar worked just as well as sugar, depending on the person he was interviewing. He noted either caution or concern in the man's voice. He figured that sugar was least likely to cause the man to hang up.

"Kyle Hosteller. Is that an American name?"

Again the long pause. "I was born in the States, but I haven't lived there in some time. You called about ...?"

To the point, Grant thought. "We're investigating the death of an American woman in Paris. A murder. Her death appears to be at the hands of a professional hit man, one with a distinct signature."

Impatiently, "And what does that have to do with us?"

Too impatiently, Grant thought. "Your sales representative appears to have been killed by the same hit man."

"And you know that for sure." Even from the other end of the line the hint of sarcasm was obvious.

"Yes, Mr. Hosteller, we do know that for sure." That was a bit of an exaggeration on his part, but Grant wasn't going to be intimidated by Mr. Hosteller. He glanced up to see that Jill had picked up her phone and was listening in on the conversation. In the back of his mind he stored the fact that the phone had not clicked when she came on-line. Special phones? "We were wondering if we could find a link between the two deaths that would help us track down the killer."

"There is no link."

Much too fast of a response with much too little information, Grant noted. "We would like to be as sure of that as you seem to be. Is there any chance we could get together to discuss this?"

"None at all. We've been in contact with the police. We believe that the death of Mr. de Bienne has nothing to do with the company. We feel it would be a waste of our time to cooperate with your organization, which has absolutely no authority when it comes to investigating the death of a French national working for a European company."

"That seems to be an extreme response for a request to meet."

"We are a company that depends on its good reputation for success. We represent an impressive list of international clients. Even a hint of scandal could be devastating to us. Link our company name to professional hit men and you will indeed regret it."

Ignoring the threat, Grant asked, "Would Walter Sutherlin be one of your clients?"

"Good day, Mr. Reynolds." The line went dead.

Grant and Jill replaced the receivers to their phones at the same time. Grant leaned back in his chair and put his feet on his desk. Jill walked over and sat on the corner of his desk. "Those aren't cowboy boots?" she asked.

"Just boots," he said.

"You're not going to go clothes-kinky on me now, are you?"

"This is what I felt like wearing when I got up today," he said. "Who knows? Tomorrow I may feel like wearing a tux."

In front of him on the desk was the notepad he used when he was on the phone. This one was covered with observations he had made while talking with Hosteller. Jill was reading the notes, although they were upside down to her. "American, late thirties or early forties, well-educated, probing, shaken. You got all of that from the phone call?"

"I didn't expect a return call from Euro-Arts. That I got one meant that someone was pretty upset about Augustus de Bienne's death. He wouldn't have called if he hadn't been shaken by his death, and I suspect he called because he was curious. U.S. Embassy. Legal Attaché. Legitimate businesses might be curious about a call from an embassy, but most wouldn't know what a Legal Attaché would be. Did you notice the one question he didn't ask?"

"What is a Legal Attaché?"

"Exactly. He didn't want to know who we were. He wanted to know what we were doing. If this company is international, if it represents people in influential places, and if it is doing anything even a tad illegal, then I suspect Mr. Hosteller knows quite well that Legal Attaché equates with FBI."

"Which would explain the quick denial and the abrupt end to the conversation."

"I suspect from here on out we'll be dealing with 'don't call us and we won't call you.'"

"Which leaves you at square one."

"No, not square one. Before the phone call, I didn't have Kyle Hosteller's name."

"I haven't got anything better to do this morning. Why don't you let me find out what I can about him?"

"Be my guest. I'm going back on-line to see if I missed anything about Euro-Arts."

Which was what Grant was doing when the second surprise of the day took place a little over an hour later. The office door opened and an attractive woman walked in.

Grant glanced at Jill after he watched the woman come in; he was interested in her response. He saw in her face an expression he had seen before: it was the one used by a woman when sizing up another. This was the same look he sometimes saw in men, especially among competitive men. It was the look of a woman spotting a rival.

He turned back to take in what generated this reaction. Grant smiled as he slowly rose from his desk to greet the woman. She was as different from Jill as ice cream was to cake. Jill was the cake with rich frosting. This woman was ice cream; name your favorite flavor and she was it. She wasn't as tall as Jill, nor was she full-figured like his colleague. No, she was what so many women wanted to be. She had narrow hips and long, shapely legs. Her stomach was flat and her breasts were small but full. She had the kind of body that would look as spectacular in a pair of cutoffs and a tank top as it would look in an expensive evening gown. Her hair was blonde, hanging in a lovely, carefully arranged tangle around her baby-doll face, complete with cherry lips and lilac-colored eyes.

She walked to Grant, smiled a fashion-model smile, slowly folded her arms around his neck, and pulled his lips down to hers. Grant let his hands slide down to her hips and just for a moment let the memories flow. The two of them had, in the past, some special moments together.

Jill's voice, with just a tinge of frost to it, said, "I think I need an introduction."

Linda Ebenhart let the kiss linger on a bit before she broke away from Grant, gathered herself together, and then offered a hand to Jill. "My name is Linda Ebenhart. I'm a representative of Mr. Walter Sutherlin."

Grant, smiling to himself, rolled his chair from behind his desk and offered it to Linda. Coincidence happened more often than we suspect, he reminded himself. On the other hand, he wasn't as surprised as Jill was by the pronouncement. That Linda Ebenhart was a representative for Walter Sutherlin didn't surprise him at all. She was a woman destined to be drawn to power and money.

They had spent three years in Harvard Law School together, graduating at the same time. Because Grant had dragged out his schooling, he was ahead of her until the end. Linda relied on him to help her get through.

She did need help, too. Intelligent and quick-witted, she was a fair student but not a gifted one. She seemed to accept her place in the middle of the pack in law school. On the other hand, she was impressed that Grant finished in the top ten percent. Linda respected a man's potential for making money.

She sat down in the chair and crossed her legs, tugging into place a conservative skirt that came down just below her knees. The dark gray skirt matched a lightweight jacket. Beneath that was a modest white blouse. She would fit nicely into the cast of a television show about lawyers. She would be the pretty one with the fashionable but conservative taste in clothes.

"What brings you here?" Grant asked.

She was great at making eye contact, and she did with both Jill and Grant as she answered, drawing them both into the conversation. "I'm in Paris to help the family with the paperwork to ship the body of poor Tiffany back to the States for burial. The family, of course, is devastated, totally unable to cope with any details."

Grant had lost track of Linda after graduation, but in reality it had begun before then. For awhile they had been torrid lovers, but that came to a slow, mutual ending after a weekend they had spent at her parents' vacation home in the Hamptons along with a dozen other guests. By the end of the weekend, Grant had noticed two things of interest. First, it was clear that her parents only tolerated Grant because he was a Harvard law student. Second, Linda spent the weekend introducing him to everyone as a homicide detective and not as a law student. He suspected that this was as close to rebellious as Linda would ever get, sleeping with a cop.

After that weekend, they both became too busy with studies to spend much time together. Nor were they ever intimate again. The last time they made love was between the silk sheets in the guest bedroom of her parents' multi-million dollar resort home. Grant had missed the sex, but he hadn't missed the twisted relationship that had little to do with love.

"I didn't know you worked for Sutherlin," Grant said.

"I've been with Walter for a little over a year now. I was equally surprised when I found out you were in Paris. I'm still not quite sure what you do." She smiled as she said this, but Grant knew a statement meant to probe when he heard one.

"Actually, I work for the State Department. My current assignment is acting as a representative for the Legal Attaché's Office."

"Does that make you a spy or a country cop or what?"

"The Legal Attaché is an FBI agent. I do investigative work for his office. I'm not a cop, nor an agent, and certainly not a spy. In the case of Tiffany Sutherby, I'm a homicide investigator."

"So you're sort of doing the same thing, only on more glamorous turf."

"Sort of. On the other hand, the turf belongs to someone else, and I don't have the same kind of authority I had."

"Except now you're backed by the U.S. government instead of the City of Boston."

"That's one way of looking at it." He knew Linda about as well as anyone would know Linda. In bed she wasn't very inventive, and she demanded satisfaction. In her social life, she expected to rub elbows with the fortunate, and she had little time for the unfortunate. In work she expected a good salary with the least difficult amount of effort to earn it. She was, to him, transparent. He had no doubt in his mind that she had been sent by Walter Sutherlin to find out exactly where Grant Reynolds fit into a political system that he was very good at manipulating. "Anything else I can tell you?"

She smiled her disarming, sincere smile. "Walter wants to know why you want to talk to him."

Linda was also someone who would take pride in being able to call a billionaire by his first name. She wasn't the type to sleep her way to the top, though. If she worked directly for Walter, then Walter saw an advantage to having a woman with a Harvard law degree who was supremely ornamental as well. Grant could imagine Linda sitting on Walter's right at a board meeting, and he could also imagine that few eyes would be on Walter when she did.

"The man who killed his granddaughter is a hired assassin. We can't find a reason that someone would want to have Tiffany killed, considering the price this killer commands, so we are exploring other possibilities."

"Such as?"

"We are looking in lots of different directions for a connection," Grant said. "Walter is one of those directions."

"He'd prefer you didn't," she said, the smile still there. "He assures you that this is not related to him. In fact, he suspects that his granddaughter was an innocent victim."

Grant looked from Linda to Jill to see how she was responding to this. One glance was enough. Jill still hadn't gotten past the kiss. "Then he believes that Escobar Saldano was the intended victim?"

"Yes."

"I'd love to see some proof to support that."

"He has the proof, but unfortunately it was gained through confidence and he cannot share it."

"And I'm to take him at his word?"

"You wouldn't want to be accused of calling Walter Sutherlin a liar."

Grant walked from his desk to the window, and then he turned back so that he was standing behind Jill. He had done it for a reason. He wanted Linda to see that this wasn't a game played just between Linda and Grant. "I wouldn't think of calling Walter a liar. As soon as I can confirm his information from a second source, I'll be able to assure him his source is reliable. Anything else?"

She re-crossed her legs, drawing his attention to them, and then she smiled. She knew what affect she had on men, although he doubted that she really understood what it was. She could abandon herself to gratification, but she couldn't abandon herself to passion. Without being able to understand her own passion, he doubted that she could understand another's.

"One more question. Still not married?"

"No. And you?"

"Still looking," she said.

He doubted that she was in much of a hurry. At thirty, she looked twenty-five. Sutherlin probably paid her an incredible salary, but even that wouldn't mean much. She would have come into a trust fund left by her grandparents by now that would have made her wealthy. Behind that was her parents' fortune. A man would have to have a hell of a lot to offer her before she would settle down. The lot would have to include wealth, power, prestige, and position. Grant had been a toy she played with once. He didn't doubt for a minute that she would play with him again, and he didn't doubt that she would discard him when she was tired of the play.

"You can tell Mr. Sutherlin that we're working hard on this case. We hope to find the killer and unravel the mystery behind the murders. You can assure him that I personally want to see this murder solved."

She stood up. Nodding to Jill, she said, "It's been a pleasure. I'll pass on the message to Walter. You'll have to forgive him if he's too busy to talk to you directly now. He's involved in the funeral arrangements back home."

Jill finally found her voice. "Will you be returning with the family?"

"The family and the body will be flying back on a chartered jet this afternoon, but I'll be staying on. Walter has asked me to keep him apprised of the investigation. I'm sure we'll be seeing quite a bit of each other." She turned to Grant and said, "I have a suite at the Hôtel Balzac. Perhaps we can have dinner. Call me." She smiled at both of them and then let herself out of the office.

As soon as the door closed, Jill asked, "Why do I suspect that you've already seen quite a bit of her?"

Still standing behind Jill, Grant scratched the back of his neck. He was never comfortable with questions that had no good answers. "We were in law school together."

She looked up at him. "And what else were you in together?"

Grant moved back to his desk. "I think we need to find out why Walter was so quick to send one of his representatives to see us," he said.

"That's what I thought," Jill said.

FIFTEEN

He was sitting in his atrium admiring his orchids to the gentle trickling murmur of his indoor fountain when his cell phone rang. He smiled because he was sure he knew who was calling him.

"I was expecting your call," he said when he answered the phone.

"Was that necessary?"

"An undervalued employee occasionally has to do something to get his employer's attention, *non?*"

"But that?"

"What better way to get across the message that I don't like the way I've been treated. If you haven't figured it out yet, I resent being at your beck and call, I resent being told that I made a mistake when the task was carried out to perfection, and I resent being told that because of it I must work at less than my negotiated fee. I also resent this rather long gap between jobs."

The other man's voice betrayed irritation, but it did not have in it a hint of fear or panic. The Assassin expected nothing less. His employee was as good at what he did as the Assassin was at what he did.

"Your action has brought some unwanted attention to us."

"The police? Please. This is hardly the most efficient organization on earth, and it is one with a very short attention span."

"Not the French, the Americans. We received a call from an employee of the Legal Attaché's Office."

He twirled the stem of a wineglass with his fingers. A fine red wine before bed was just the right touch for a good night's sleep. "FBI?" he asked.

"Not an agent. Some kind of a field representative."

"A petty governmental minion?"

"I don't know who he is. His name is Grant Reynolds and he's new."

The wineglass stopped spinning. "You know nothing more about him?"

"No. Just his name. You have gotten us in a mess."

With a flip of his hand, the wine glass arched across the atrium and came crashing down in the lower bowl of the tiered fountain, sending glass shards into the water. "I don't seem to be getting through to you. I did not make a mess. I did what you asked me to do. This is not the first time you have chosen a highly visible target, and with that comes the kind of 'mess' you so describe. I'll clean up *your* mess for you, but each person I must eliminate to do it will cost you the normal fee."

"Why should I pay for your mistakes?" The man's voice rose, but the Assassin could tell that it was show and not from any great change in emotion.

"Because I know who you are, I know where you live, and I know your habits. You will respect our agreement or you will join de Bienne."

This time the emotion was genuine. "Are you threatening me?"

"You are so busy protecting yourself that you seem to overlook the fact that I must protect myself as well. If I think you are going to do something stupid that could lead back to me, I will not think twice about eliminating you."

"Let's not be foolish," he said.

"I am never foolish."

"Excuse me, but that congresswoman in the grocery store—"

"*Pardon moi,* but that was a few years ago, and I'm still walking the streets a free man. If that is your reason for cutting back on my services, then I feel the need to correct you."

The voice was calmer now. "That's far from the reason. With the stock markets so volatile of late, we don't have as many clients as we had in the past. With fewer clients, we've had fewer problems."

"I'll accept that for now, but I would hate to find out that my services have been contracted out to another."

"I assure you that won't happen."

"And I assure that I will take care of any problems that come up."

The line went dead. Except for the toss of the wineglass, no one observing this conversation would have suspected anger on the Assassin's part. He was an expert at masking his emotions. He poured some more wine into a second glass on the tray next to his chair. Cleaning up the mess they made would come later, but now he had a more pressing problem. Grant Reynolds. When he could, the Assassin followed the aftermath of one of his kills by logging on to newspaper Internet sites. He had read extensively about the frustration following the death of the congresswoman with a certain satisfaction. The name of Grant Reynolds had come up often in the stories. A homicide detective, he was the first to make the link between this killing and others done by a man who had become known to Interpol as the Assassin.

Grant Reynolds, he learned from his reading, was not just another dumb cop. He was educated, intelligent, and dedicated. He would hate to think that this was the same

Grant Reynolds who now worked for the U.S. government. He could be a challenging adversary. He smiled to himself. But of course, he would kill Reynolds long before he became a challenging adversary.

SIXTEEN

Grant had only been out of bed for a few minutes when his cell phone rang. He answered it, expecting Jill on the other end of the call. He was wrong. Linda's cheerful voice greeted him.

"Good morning, Grant. I hope I didn't wake you."

"No, Linda, I'm already up. How did you get this number?" This was a secure line, and the number was only used by people connected to the embassy.

"Walter Sutherlin can do just about anything, including getting your cell phone number."

Perhaps he could, Grant thought, but that would entail a contact with an aide to Sutherlin's friend in the White House, which in turn would require a series of calls through diplomatic channels, culminating in someone from the embassy calling Linda and giving her his phone number. Grant was not impressed by the maneuvering through channels. Instead he was curious why Sutherlin would go to all the trouble.

"Do you think he could get me a nice apartment in the center of Paris for eight hundred dollars a month?"

"I'm sure he could," she said, "but then he would own you. You're not the type to be owned."

He let that ride. He wasn't interested in pursuing a conversation that would lead them into an analysis of their failed relationship. "What are you doing up so early?" he asked to change the subject.

"I just got back from my jog. Paris is a beautiful place for a jogger. Lots of paths for running here. I finished with a sprint back to my hotel."

"That explains why you're still so fit and trim," he said, leaving it at that. He really didn't want to think about her body, which was as close to perfection as he had seen in a female body.

"I'm glad you noticed. By the way, I called to invite you to dinner tonight."

He knew he should say no, but he also knew that this was as close to Walter Sutherlin as he was likely to get. "I'm free this evening."

"Good. My hotel at eight. It has a lovely restaurant."

"You want me to meet you where?"

"I'll wait for you in the lobby."

"I'll be there," he said.

"Lovely," she said and hung up.

"Lovely," he said to himself. "Two old friends getting together to try to use each other."

He finished dressing and descended to the dining room for breakfast. He went from there directly to work.

He had dressed in a sports coat and tie because it was a Friday, and it felt like a sports coat and tie kind of day. A fortunate choice. When he walked into the office, Dale Bailey, sitting at his desk, inspected Grant from head to foot before saying, "Good morning. I was hoping I'd catch you before Jill came in."

That was a leading statement, Grant thought, as he slipped off his sports coat and draped it over the back of his chair before taking a seat at his own desk. "I suppose there's a reason for that."

"First let me say that I've been impressed in the short time you've been here. You definitely are a professional.

On the other hand, I feel I need to remind you that being a professional policeman and being a professional government employee are not necessarily the same thing."

Grant had wondered how long it would take before he would hear a speech like this. Walter Sutherlin was certainly exerting some pressure, and he wouldn't be surprised if the folks at Euro-Arts weren't pushing some buttons as well. "I would think that regardless of the profession, both jobs would seek the same thing—a solution to a problem." He left it cryptic to see how Dale would respond.

"I've received a call from the ambassador himself. He, too, is impressed with your professionalism. He did, though, ask me to remind you that a derivative of the word diplomat is diplomacy."

Cute. A fatherly reminder from his kindly ambassador. "Have I done something wrong?" Grant asked.

Dale held up a hand. "No, no, no," he said. "Not at all. You've been asked to collect information for the Legat Office about the murder of Tiffany Sutherby, and you've done an exceptional job of that. I can understand your desire to talk to Walter Sutherlin, and in a murder investigation I'm sure you've had to find a balance between your need to know and a family's grief. Right now Mr. Sutherlin is consumed with grief, and has no time to talk to you. Perhaps at a more appropriate time."

But he had time to get my cell phone number. "I certainly wouldn't want to intrude at an inappropriate time," Grant said.

"That's exactly what I told the ambassador," Dale said, smiling like a patriarch.

Thanks for the lecture, Dad, and now back to business. "Are you back with us now?" he asked.

"Actually, I'm only here for the morning. Following the counterfeit money proved to be the right thing to do. We were able to link the trail of the money to the itinerary of an American tourist. The police have made an arrest."

And you have a nice tan, Grant wanted to add. Trailing counterfeit money must be rewarding. "Congratulations," he said.

"Thanks. I can't take a lot of the credit. The police were very cooperative."

"What next for you, then? You did say you would only be with us for the morning."

"Oh, right. Actually, I'm picking up on something you started, the American who's suspected of illegally selling computer equipment to the Russians. I'm off to London. The Legat Office there has been looking into this as well. We're launching a joint effort."

If he had started the case, shouldn't he be the one to go off to London? Grant wanted to ask. He didn't ask, of course. Dale was the type who might cave in to such reason and send Grant out of guilt. The last thing that Grant wanted was for Dale to be hanging around any more than he had to, especially if he was the designated deliverer of fatherly advice.

"This would be a nice time to visit London," Grant said.

"Yes, a lovely time," Dale said, failing to suspect even a hint of sarcasm.

When Jill arrived a little later, she didn't seem pleased to see either one of them. Grant stayed out of harm's way as Jill and Dale huddled at his desk to review what had taken place while he was gone. Grant did notice that Jill did not look his way once. He had learned a long time ago that women were odd creatures, and he wasn't born one of those lucky men who would easily understand them.

He was left to man the office when Dale and Jill went to lunch. He wasn't invited to tag along. He considered that fortunate when Gerard called.

The inspector filled him in on de Bienne's murder. "I have no doubt that the man was killed by the Assassin. Everything fits, right down to the hat the man was wearing. By the way, we are continuing to look into that through Interpol. So far those who noticed describe either the hat you have in the picture James Smith had made up, or one very similar to it."

"Do you have any theories as to why de Bienne was killed?" Grant asked.

"Nothing in his personal life offers a reason. He was not a drug user, he did not have a mistress, he was not sleeping with another's wife, he did not have unpaid gambling debts ... . He truly was rather unimaginative. Good food, movies, nice clothes: most of his income went to his family, which included a wife and three children in private schools. About the only gift he seems to have had was arranging sales of artwork and writing contracts for those sales, and was only moderately good at that, considering the few commissions he got from his work. On the other hand, a commission for a sale on two million Euro is enough to support a lifestyle like his on the number of sales he made."

"Then it would be a good guess that the murder was related perhaps to his work and not his private life."

"That is what we are looking into."

"What have you discovered about Euro-Arts?"

"Very little. I've talked to a Kyle Hosteller, who seems to be the representative for the company, but I've yet to talk to anyone higher than he."

"Is there someone higher up?" Grant asked.

Gerard thought about that for a moment before answering. "I suspect yes. The firm has so cloaked itself in secrecy that I can't be sure."

"Hosteller called me," Grant said.

"As he did me," Gerard replied. "I thought the call might

be pre-emptive. Call the police and then they won't look too hard into your business while trying to reach you."

"I also thought Hosteller was trying to deflect our interest. He was also threatening. Pushed too hard, and he knows some people in high places, that kind of thing."

"He was much nicer to me. I suspect Americans don't scare him, but Europeans do. I'm not sure why, yet. I think he might fear we have a key that could unlock his secrets."

"Do you?"

The inspector laughed. "I don't know."

"What I would really like to have," Grant said, "is a look at Euro-Arts' client list. I suspect the names on it will either link Sutherlin or the Saldanos to the murders. Any suggestions?"

"You need to talk to James Smith at Interpol. I think you will find, if you find it at all, that the client list is so layered under misdirection that only a computer expert in mazes and subterfuge would have a chance to get those names for you."

"Hats and a list of names. On the surface it seems simple enough."

"It is all part of the glamour of police work."

"Thanks for the update. If I learn anything useful, I'll get back to you."

"I would like to say that I can do the same for you, but you know the nature of diplomacy ..."

Grant knew more about it than he had a week ago. He thanked the inspector again and then hung up. He finished writing some reports that he had put off to be sent to the Legat Office, and then he locked up the office to go down to the bar on the corner for a bite to eat and a beer.

Again, Grant was reminded of how much he loved the French attitude toward drinking. No one seemed to think twice about having a glass of beer or wine during working hours. Drinking on the job in the States could get you in a lot of trouble, but in France, like Jill had said at lunch that day, not drinking could be a social faux pas. He was beginning to like Paris even more.

When he returned to the office, Jill was there but Dale was gone. As he made himself comfortable at his desk, he asked Jill, "Has he gone again?"

She glanced up briefly from a paper she was reading and said, "He truly loves having you in the office. It has given him a license to flee. He's been set free. I doubt seriously that we will see any more of him than we have this week."

"Won't that raise an eyebrow at the Legat Office?"

"Dale is a wonder boy. He has this incredible ability to attach himself to cases that are close to resolution, ones that are being wrapped up by the local police or by another Legat Office, and he is able to be there in the end and take a little bit of the credit. I'm sure the Legal Attaché has his own private thoughts about Dale, but the man's record on paper cannot be ignored. Besides, we now have you."

There was something in the way she said the last statement that suggested it wasn't a compliment. "You mean you have more manpower than before, so Dale's wanderings aren't as crucial as they might have been," he said.

"I mean the Legal Attaché is impressed by the fact that in only a week you are receiving high praise from both the French police and Interpol, and even Walter Sutherlin has sent an executive assistant to speak to you personally." From the look on her face, he could tell that this perception of the Legal Attaché did not please her.

"You and Dale must have had quite a conversation," he said.

"Actually, Dale and the Legal Attaché had quite a conversation, with the ambassador sitting in."

"That we are doing our job isn't a bad perception for them to have."

"That *you* are doing *your* job is the perception they have," she said.

Now he understood. She felt that he was making her look bad. "I'm not trying to be a glory hound," he said. "I don't care who gets credit for what. Right now my priority is to get the Assassin."

She seemed to relax a little. "I'm not accusing you of showboating," she said. "You might notice, though, that all the names mentioned have been those of men. I'm sort of looked on as a glorified secretary by the Legat Office."

"Then help me catch the Assassin and take the credit," Grant said.

"Right, and how am I going to do that?"

"I need a list of Euro-Arts' clients. I think that information might be the key, eventually, to solving the murder of Tiffany Sutherby."

She started to say something sarcastic. "Wait, I think I have that list in my purse ..." Then she stopped. "It's not only the FBI and Interpol that try to track art, several other agencies do, as well. There are private organizations paid to verify the authenticity of pieces of art. I might walk to the Louvre and see if I can find someone there who has some ideas. If we can identify artwork brokered by Euro-Arts, we might be able to trace that to buyers, and from those buyers ultimately to a list of other buyers. It's a long shot," she said, rising from her desk, "but ..." She grabbed her purse and was out the door.

Grant smiled to himself. The two of them would be spending a lot of time working across a room from each other, regardless of where their social lives went. He knew it would be important to keep her happy if he was going to get his job done in peace. And she looked pretty happy when she rushed out the door.

By the time Jill came back, Grant was quite pleased with himself. He had received two calls while she was gone. One was from a travel coordinator for a senior citizens group in Florida, requesting information about a French tour guide company. The second was a call from a law firm in the Midwest that was trying to track down a French national, a distant relative of an American who had left a bequest for the person in his will.

With a very limited French vocabulary, Grant wasn't about to tackle these himself. At first he thought he would leave them for Jill, and then he reconsidered. He needed to carry his own weight even with the little things.

He called the one person he thought could help him, one who spoke pretty good English: Gerard's secretary. He explained, that no, he didn't want to speak to the inspector but to her. She seemed flattered. He told her about the two requests he had received. Within a few minutes she had given him the name and number of an agency, not unlike the Better Business Bureau in America, that the travel coordinator could contact, and she gave him the number of a woman who worked in vital statistics who spoke fluent English.

He thanked her profusely, and then he made the second call. There he was able to find an address and phone number of the person mentioned in the will. He then called back the tour coordinator and law office with the information he had received. As a final thought, he ducked out of the office and walked a block and half to a flower shop and arranged for a bouquet to be sent to Gerard's secretary with a card expressing his thanks.

As a homicide detective, he had developed a network

of informants to help him get his job done. Now he was beginning to log a list of names and numbers of people who could help him get his job done in Paris. The two ideas were not so far from each other. A man needed a support group to get through life, whether or not it was in the work world or in his personal life.

He noted, too, wryly, that he had yet to meet the stereotypic rude Parisian. So far the only rude people he had run across in Paris were Americans. He also noted, again wryly, that the embassy sent to them requests that should be handled someplace else. He suspected the workers there did it because of ignorance. They didn't know where else to send it. Grant decided he would start compiling a list of resources and agencies—including names of people who spoke English and their phone numbers—to send over to the embassy. Gently at first, he was determined to change the image of the office he worked in as the dumping ground for unwanted work. He wanted the office to become, in time, a serious investigative unit with a larger staff, better facilities, and more clout.

He was sure that Dale would see him as overly ambitious. If so, he didn't know Grant very well. Every time he had gone into a job, it had been with a goal in mind. When he left homicide in Boston, his department was a much better organized and more efficient operation. He saw no reason the same thing couldn't happen here. He was very much a believer that change had to come from within.

When Jill returned, she was happily humming to herself. When she settled in behind her desk, she said to Grant, "I talked to one of the assistant directors at the Louvre. I got some great leads on galleries and even insurance companies that try to track the movements of artwork. She also provided me with several national organizations that do the same thing in England, France, and Germany. The

Europeans are serious about the preservation of art; they do their best to keep track of an artwork's provenance."

"That works well for old art, but what about works by new painters?" Grant asked.

"Surprisingly, if the painter has a reputation, the same applies. The artwork is tracked from its first sale. As the director explained, she's saving someone one hundred years from now from the difficulties she has trying to keep track of artwork created centuries ago."

"Let's hope that Euro-Arts plays by the rules when it comes to helping track art."

"I'll know in a few days. Many of these organizations have Internet sites. I think we're making progress. How would you like to go to dinner to celebrate?"

He knew he could turn this into an awkward moment for both of them, but he was determined not to. "I'll have to take a rain check," he said. "Linda called me this morning and invited me to dinner. I see it as an opportunity to find out more about Sutherlin."

Jill held her smile, but some light went out of her eyes. "Maybe another time, then," she said.

"How about tomorrow night?" he asked.

"Are you sure Linda won't have some other plans?" she asked.

"Linda and I had a relationship once. It ended for some really good reasons. None of those reasons have changed. I suspect that whatever plans Linda might have may well be Walter Sutherlin's plans. I think he wants to know as much about us as we want to know about him. I'm not going to trip over myself providing Linda an opportunity to get that information."

"You mean no pillow talk?"

"It's a little early between us to get jealous," he said with a smile, "but I kind of like the idea that you might be."

She laughed. "Don't hold your breath. You could invite me to go to dinner with the two of you."

"The way you two sparked yesterday? No way. You'll just have to settle for hearing it secondhand tomorrow night."

"How about dinner on the Eiffel Tower?"

"You can do that?" he asked.

"On the first level the restaurants are open year-round."

"That sounds romantic."

"Don't expect to get lucky twice in one weekend."

"Funny, I don't expect to get lucky once."

SEVENTEEN

It did not help to put the past to rest when Grant spotted Linda in the hotel lobby. She was wearing a dress so formfitting that no curve of her body went unnoticed. He had to give her credit. Without either a plunging neckline or a revealing slit up the side of her dress, she still had every man who walked through the lobby drooling by the time he reached the other side. He was glad he'd chosen to wear his best suit with a tie or he might well have disappeared standing next to her.

No quick kisses on the cheek for Linda. As soon as he got close enough she wrapped him into her arms and gave him a full-body hug that brought back some very fond memories. "Why did we ever break up?" she asked in his ear.

They both knew quite well why they broke up. Her parents weren't enamored with the idea of their daughter running around with a commoner, but they tolerated it because he was near the top of his class in Harvard Law School. That tolerance quickly faded when he let them know that he either would not practice law at all when he got his degree, or he would work as a prosecuting attorney. It didn't help, either, during the weekend he spent with her parents, that he told Linda's father, irritated because the man was pushing him to consider working for a prestigious law firm, that he was about as interested in money as he was in expensive houses in resort communities.

Grant wasn't so opposed to money that he gave his away, but in his experience money bought "things" that then led to ulcers, trouble, dissatisfaction, or crime.

Her father had suggested that there was something un-American about such an attitude. Grant had replied that he might be un-capitalistic but not un-Christian. That had sealed the fate of his relationship with Linda. She listened to mom and dad.

He extricated himself from her, more concerned about walking into the restaurant with a bulge in his pants than hurting her feelings. "Did you notice the lust level rise in this room when you walked into it?" he asked.

"Only mine when you walked in the room," she said. "How is it that as you get older you get more handsome?"

"I only date women with failing eyesight," he said.

"And I see you still remain modest," she said.

"If I thought myself handsome or I thought myself modest, flattery might work," he said. "Why don't we go eat? Unlike you fashionable folks, I'm used to eating early."

She took him by the hand and led him toward the dining room. He noticed two things along the way. The men they passed looked at him with a certain respect, and the women looked at him with interest. Drape a beautiful woman on your arm and your worth skyrockets, he thought, especially in a four-star hotel. For some reason, he didn't think he would see the same reaction in his hotel.

She insisted on ordering for both of them, claiming that she still remembered his tastes and also that she knew the chef. He didn't question either statement. People like Linda would always want to order, and they would always know the chef. She selected duck breasts with cassis and raspberries, along with mushrooms a la grecque. All very tasty, but not what he would have chosen.

Not until the meal was coming to an end did they get down to business. Grant had been expecting it. When they'd separated years before, he doubted that Linda had cried too many tears. He was diversion until she got to real life. He not only doubted that she'd maintained a secret passion for him, but he even doubted that she'd given him much thought until his name came up in the investigation of Tiffany Sutherby's death.

He did allow himself to relax over a second glass of wine and to poke fun at himself. Here he was with an incredibly beautiful woman who was practically throwing herself at him, and he doubted for a moment that it was his good looks and charm that were responsible for it. He broke the spell of the evening himself.

"What does Walter want to know?" he asked.

Linda nearly choked on a sip of wine. "Excuse me?" she asked when she could finally get the words out.

"Since we last saw each other, you have not once looked back over your shoulder to see where I might have gone, and now you suddenly find me the most fascinating man on earth."

She gave him a hard look, and then she smiled. "I didn't use to be quite so transparent, did I?" she asked.

"You probably were, but I was so fascinated with your body at the time I may have missed it."

That caused her to giggle. "In bed was where we had most of our fun."

"I couldn't argue with that," he said, tipping his wineglass to her before taking a drink.

"As you've already figured out, this dinner isn't all pleasure."

"Good," Grant said. "We can charge it to your business expenses."

She shook her head, still smiling. "You're the most

unusual man I have ever known," she said. "Of course this will go on my business expense sheet."

"Now that we have that out of the way, what does Walter want to know?"

"He wants to know the direction your investigation is taking," she said. He noticed that a little bit of the charm disappeared as the lawyer in her came out.

"He wants to know if the investigation is coming in his direction," Grant said.

"Walter is consumed with grief. He has neither the energy nor the desire to talk to you right now, especially since he believes this has nothing to do with him."

And Walter has never lied to anyone on his way to his billions of dollars. "For now, I'm still trying to find out who the intended victim was. I'm assuming that one of them was in the wrong place at the wrong time. Until I know that, I really can't focus on an investigation. I'm still into fact finding."

"Walter has authorized me to answer any questions I can for him."

That was about as good as secondhand smoke, but for the moment Grant doubted he was going to get any closer to Walter than this. "How close was he to Tiffany?"

"Grant, you have to promise that whatever I say here stays here. You know what a tabloid would do with any juicy information pertaining to Walter."

He spread the lapels of his jacket. "See, no tape recorder."

She accepted that, a little too quickly Grant thought. Walter must have a slant on this that he desperately wanted Grant to believe. "He was not close to Tiffany at all, which is why it would make little sense to kill her if someone was trying to get to Walter. She's always been a problem child, requiring the family lawyers to bail her out time and time again. What's on her official record is only a small part of the trouble she got into. Two abortions, drug rehabilitation, money that simply flowed through her fingers and disappeared, overcharges, over-indulgences; you name it and she was good at it. On top of that, she hated her grandfather for being rich, and in her words, for being stingy. If you were out to hurt him, Tiffany wasn't a very good target."

"Maybe she was the only one available."

She swirled wine in her glass and then said, "Hardly. Walter has three daughters; he is proud of none of them. He has—or had—three granddaughters. The one redeeming grace of God in his eyes is that his last daughter had a grandson who's doing graduate studies at Stanford in the school of business. If you wanted to hurt him, this's where you'd aim."

"I thought Tiffany's father was the heir apparent," Grant said.

"Scott is the stop-gap until Larry is ready to join the company."

"How does Scott feel about that?"

"Even after he's edged out by Larry, Scott will be making more money than he ever dreamed of. No hard feelings there."

"Then don't you think someone might have targeted Tiffany because they didn't know all of this?"

"I think if someone went to all the trouble to target Tiffany, they would have learned along the way that she wasn't in good standing with her grandfather, her father, or her mother. The sheep don't get much blacker than her."

"Is there anything else I'm supposed to know?" he asked.

"Don't be so cynical," she snapped.

Will the real Linda Ebenhart please come down? "Excuse me if I appear that way, but when you go to a press conference where the speaker doesn't show, and you're given answers to the questions, but you don't get to ask the questions, then cynical might be the right word. I'm investigating a murder. I'd like to think that all parties would like to see it solved."

"Not if any of the parties might be embarrassed by the solution," she said.

"Because of Tiffany's previous behavior?"

"Walter would like to protect as much of her memory as he can."

"Admirable for a man who didn't approve of her."

"He was still her grandfather."

They could continue to joust, but Grant was sure that he'd been given the information he was to have: Tiffany was such a bad girl that even grandpa couldn't love her. Killing her would hardly be the thing to do to make Grandpa feel bad. Whatever Grant might be thinking about the causes for the murder, they had nothing to do with Walter. Back off. Get lost. To soften the words, he had sent a very beautiful woman to say them.

"How about dessert? Does that go on your expense account, too?"

Linda knew Grant well enough to know that the business conversation had come to an end. She had seen him close up and watched him crawl into himself before. He thought that money had been the reason they'd separated, but that wasn't it at all. She had never loved a man as deeply as she had loved him. But he came with a protective wrapping, and she, after nearly two years of trying, hadn't found a way past it. She wondered if he had even a clue about the truth of their relationship.

He ate his dessert, cinnamon bavarois, feeling, as he concentrated on the delicacy, the intensity of Linda's stare. Each time he glanced up, she was still staring at him. She was lost somewhere behind her eyes, so he doubted she even knew she was staring at him. He was a little curious, but he didn't give it much thought. When they had been together before, she had occasionally looked at him the same way. He wondered then if she was measuring the man against his potential and in the end found the potential wanting.

To break this spell, and without looking up, he asked, "Is there a man in your life?"

The stare broke, and her eyes crinkled into a smile. "Why, I didn't think you cared."

"And why do I think you're avoiding the question?"

She was. She didn't want him to know that she had yet to find a man who interested her as much as he had. "I've gone through a few, but I've yet to find one who would stick."

"Your problem or his?"

That mind of his could do laser surgery, she thought. "Walter keeps me busy. I travel a lot for him." She quickly redirected the course of the conversation. "Did I sense that you've got something going with the woman who works in your office?"

He wasn't surprised by the question. Women seemed to have a radar system when it came to relationships. "Give me a break. I've only been in Paris a little over a week. I don't work that fast."

"That makes us both free and single," she said, the implication obvious.

"How long do you plan to stay in Paris?" he asked.

"How long before you wrap up this case?"

"I suggest you either rent or buy, then, because this could take a while."

"Do you have a spare room?"

He watched the disbelief unfold in her features as he

told her about his room in the hotel. "If I remember right about you and clothes, my room would be smaller than your closet."

"But you do have a double bed?"

He reached across the table and patted her on the back of a hand. "I think we need to settle for our memories for the time being. You represent a client who is involved in an investigation. Professionalism dictates that we keep our distance."

"You've turned into a spoilsport," she said.

"No," he said, "I just remember that nothing in our relationship before was casual."

"Like in casual sex?"

"Exactly."

She lifted her glass of wine to her lips and over the rim of it her eyes still smiled. "I got to you back then, didn't I?"

He nodded. "You are one of those women a man doesn't forget."

She settled the glass back on the table and wrapped both hands around it, blatantly staring across the table at Grant. He was a handsome man, even with a little too much beard he had to tame each day. He had been a considerate lover, a good friend, and an excellent tutor. Still, much of him was a mystery to her. She knew about the policewoman who had died. She knew he had loved her, even though he would not admit it to himself. She knew about the nightmares he had, caused by his work. She knew that Sunday mornings were out for anything because Grant had to go to Mass, rain or shine, holiday, or test to cram for.

His faith intrigued her the most about him, in part because she did not have any. He had once said to her, "God may be indifferent but the Church is not." She never really understood what that meant, but she sensed that the Church gave some order to his life that he desperately needed. She was careful never to ridicule or question his religion.

In the end, she found him too complex to figure out. She could have made a life around him, and she could have even sacrificed her comfortable lifestyle to do it, but she was never quite as sure about him. Could he make any sacrifices for her?

"A franc for your thoughts," he said.

"With inflation, you couldn't afford my thoughts," she said, her eyes now showing a little of the sadness she felt.

After dinner, which she put on her tab, he walked her to the elevator that would take her back to her room. "You're welcome to come up for a drink," she said.

"Don't offer an alcoholic a drink," he said.

Grant was not an alcoholic and never would be, but that was the phrase he always used when she'd walk out of his bathroom naked. In bed he never could get enough of her, nor could she get enough of him. They had created some wonderful chemistry between them back then.

She put a hand behind his neck and pulled his lips down to hers, kissing him passionately. When she pulled free from him and pushed the button for the elevator, she said over her shoulder, "You're going to send a woman to bed tonight with a dull ache."

He didn't have an answer to that. He'd have a dull ache himself, but the warning bells inside said the same thing over and over again: Don't go there. He had finally learned to heed those bells.

EIGHTEEN

He got up late on Saturday morning, leaving himself just enough time to make it down to breakfast before serving was over. He had purchased a thermos just for this. He poured his coffee into it and wrapped up a croissant in the tinfoil he'd also brought down with him. With breakfast in hand, he climbed back to the lobby and headed out the front door. Around the corner was a newspaper and magazine stand. He bought a *USA Today*, printed in English, and hiked the half a dozen blocks or so to Jardin du Luxembourg.

This was one of the things he had put on his to-do list while in Paris. He wanted to get up on a sunny day, take his breakfast, and sit in one of the chairs that surrounded the grand fountain in the middle of the garden to eat his breakfast and read his newspaper. His stay in Paris was going to be full of such simple pleasures.

Children still came to this fountain to rent toy sailboats to float across the water as they had in Hemingway's day, a scene he had described in *A Moveable Feast*. Grant doubted that a whole lot had changed in that time, except the dress of the people and the fact that someone was already at the fountain trying out a radio-controlled boat. Hemingway probably would have thought that a travesty.

This was Paris in the summer, which meant that even on a sunny morning the air had a slight chill to it. He didn't mind. He faced his chair toward the sun and with the help of the coffee was warm and comfortable in short order. He had pulled up a second chair to use as a footstool, so he was relaxed and at peace. This moment was everything he imagined it would be. He sat in a faded green wrought-iron lawn chair that probably wasn't much different from the one Hemingway used to sit in. Across the tan, crushed rock was a huge, circular fountain with an urn in the middle that shot a spiral of water into the air. Beyond the fountain were benches, a stretch of grass, a line of statues that bordered the grounds, and trees. Except for the view of a tall tower in the distance, he could have been in the countryside instead of in the middle of one of the oldest cities in Europe.

Paris could be his outdoor room for the next few months, until the weather turned wet and cold. There was already a cloud on his horizon, and Grant was afraid that his hotel room would become claustrophobic. He, like the other guests, were welcome to sit in the tiny lobby of the hotel where a little more of the world passed by, or they could go back down to the dining room once it was cleaned after breakfast and sit at a table to watch television. The hotel did appear to have a cable service of some kind, but Grant knew nothing about the selection.

When the weather was really bad, he would be restricted mostly to going to his office or his room. That would be too small of a world for him, he knew. If he were to actually going to stay in Paris for a couple of years, he would have to look for something bigger, an apartment. He would not, though, settle for something on the fringes of Paris. He decided then that he would learn to read the listings for rentals and try to find a place on the Left Bank. After all, he thought, thousands of university students lived in the area. If they could afford an apartment, certainly he could, too.

An hour later Grant cleaned up after himself, tossing the newspaper and tinfoil in a trashcan in the park, and then ran the strap of the thermos through two belt loops on the back of his pants. He was ready for a hike around this part of the city, to see things he had not seen before and to look for the two things that gave him the most pleasure for the moment: books and music.

He had already discovered that Paris offered a wealth of music by artists new to him. He was a bit like a kid in a candy store. He didn't know where to start. Books were another problem. Most bookstores, many of them with bins of books out front on the sidewalk, had a good collection of titles in English. He resisted the temptation to overstock, or he might well find himself happy to be locked away in his room doing nothing more than reading and listening to music.

He knew that he was in some kind of a retreat from the life he had led before. He even understood the need for it. One didn't spend years working as a homicide detective during the nights while studying to be a lawyer during the days without burning both ends of the candle precariously close to the center. The shooting of the boy had been the final act to undo a frayed psyche. He needed to get away from it, and he needed a rest. This job seemed like the perfect solution at the time. No task too demanding. Regular hours. Paris to play in. He felt guilty when he decided to take it.

The guilt was gone. After only a little over a week in Paris, he was ready for a weekend. He needed a break. The job was more demanding than he'd thought it would be, and a murder investigation was as time-consuming here as it was in Boston. In some ways he was comforted by the familiar, but in others he worried that the rest and the healing he needed wouldn't get done here as he hoped.

Still … here he was thinking he needed an apartment to live in. He was already settling in, and he wouldn't feel that way if he didn't like it.

He took interest in a potted palm tree, the pot nearly five-feet high and the tree perhaps twenty-five-feet tall. He wondered if the tree was taken in someplace for the winter, for he had trouble imagining a palm surviving a Paris winter, but then he thought of the all the trouble that would be. Of course, that was why Paris was Paris. The people here worked very hard to keep it the way it was.

He got up and wandered toward the Luxembourg Palace, built to order by Marie de Medici, queen to Henri IV. Like most tourists, Grant had done his reading. With little else to do while her husband chased other women, the queen set her sights on being a palace-builder. He laughed at the thought. Angry at her husband's infidelities, she must have been determined to get even by spending his money. A woman scorned today would probably do the same thing.

He was unimpressed by the exterior of the building, although he imagined it would be grand inside, although in reality it's not. If he had a complaint about Paris, it was that too many of the buildings looked alike. Sometimes it was hard to tell a palace from a department store.

The sun was out and the day had turned warm. He had dressed for the chill with a sweater. He decided to walk back to his room so he could leave the sweater and thermos behind as he continued to roam the city. Back in his room, though, his plans changed. From his window, he spotted Jill at work in the office across the way. He decided to wander over and see what she was doing.

When he walked into the office, Jill looked up briefly from her computer and smiled at him, and then she went back to work. He said to her, "A beautiful Saturday morning in Paris is not the best time to be working."

Without looking up again, she said, "We don't get over-time, but we get comp time. Keep track of any extra hours you put in. The next lovely afternoon when work is slow, you can walk out the door without guilt and enjoy a stroll along the Seine. How was dinner?"

"Any dinner I don't cook myself is wonderful," he said.

"I gathered that," she said. "Are you hinting at an invitation?"

"Didn't we make plans for tonight?" he asked.

"Didn't things go well with Linda?"

Maybe it was an odd axiom for men. Women they had bedded were never quite as interesting as women they had not. When it came to Linda and Jill, he suspected this was true for him. "Things went fine," he said. "We actually had a fairly pleasant visit."

"And dessert?" Her lips were locked in a hard little smile.

"I dropped her off at her elevator. Mixing work and pleasure is never a good idea," he said, wondering how he could keep his face straight. He noted that she nodded slightly.

"Learn anything?"

"I learned that Tiffany Sutherby was a great disappointment to her grandfather, so much so that she was his least favorite grandchild, and he was not close to her. On the other hand, he was so devastated by her loss that he couldn't possibly talk to me."

"And Linda told you that with a straight face?"

"Yes she did. I think that in the billionaire's club you're expected to take them at their word, no questions asked."

"What was your take on it?"

"I was reassured emphatically that this has nothing to do with Walter."

"And ...?"

"And now I'm convinced that it has everything to do with him."

"Then you'll like this," she said, looking up from the computer. "Euro-Arts and Walter have done quite a bit of business together."

It took Jill most of the morning working through a dozen Internet sites to establish that in the last twenty years Euro-Arts had arranged dozens of purchases of significant works of art for Walter Sutherlin. So many that Jill said he must have a mini-museum located someplace.

Grant examined the list. None of the artists were at the top of the list when it came to fame, but some were very close to the top, and Walter had paid on several occasions a half a million dollars or more for a piece.

With the list still in hand, Grant asked, "What do you know about art?"

Jill made a face. "I know if I like it or not," she said.

He sighed. Was she not being helpful on purpose? Was there something about last night that still made her mad? She had ignored his attempt to invite himself to dinner. "What I was wondering was," he said, "is there some kind of plan to his acquisitions? Is he simply collecting paintings he likes, or has he got some kind of theme to his approach?"

"Would it make any difference?"

Good question, he thought. "I don't know. I'm trying to understand. We now know there's a link between Euro-Arts and Walter Sutherlin. Next we need to know if there's a link between Euro-Arts, Walter Sutherlin, and the deaths of Tiffany Sutherby and Augustus de Bienne."

"And Walter's taste in art will tell us that?" Skeptical was the least cynical description he could have given to her tone of voice.

"Work with me here," he said. "I've solved a lot of crimes

by accumulating as much information as I could about the victim. Eighty percent of the information was useless to the solution of the crime, but the odd bits of information often added up to clues that were invaluable."

She didn't look convinced. "And this isn't information you could find out for yourself?"

"Sure," he said, "if you give me the name of your contact at the Louvre."

"She doesn't speak English."

"Everyone in Paris speaks English," he said smirking, "only she speaks it about as well as I speak French. She doesn't want to embarrass herself, so she pretends she doesn't speak English."

"And you're sure of that."

"No. It's just an educated guess."

She wasn't about to admit that he was right, but he was. They had tried English first, before the assistant at the Louvre had gotten lost. "I'll talk to her again," she said, "but don't make me your gofer."

"We talked about dinner tonight," he said.

"Where?"

"You suggested the Eiffel Tower?"

"It'll probably be packed with tourists on a Saturday night," she said.

"Pigalle, then. I hear it's pretty spicy up there."

"Pigalle isn't quite as sketchy as it once was, but it still has some interesting clubs that you don't frequent alone. And it's still pretty focused on the sex industry, upscale or not. One or two clubs are not too expensive, and you can get a good dinner. I would be glad to introduce you to Pigalle," she said, "but you pay."

Although he would never be rich, he would always have enough for a night on the town. "What time do you want me to pick you up?"

"I'll come and get you about seven," she said. "Now get out of here. I want to try some more links on the Internet and you're keeping me from it."

A walk through sunny Paris on a Saturday morning beat being in the office any day. "When you get to the lobby of my hotel, have the manager ring me."

"Gee, and I thought you'd be trying to get me into your room."

"If you've seen one cheap hotel room in Paris, you've seen them all," he said as he walked out the door. He didn't want to start a conversation about his intentions. He didn't know what his intentions were; he only knew what he thought already: Mixing work and play was a dangerous practice.

When good things happened to Grant, they seemed to come from nowhere. Although he had applied for the Harvard School of Law, he hadn't expected to be accepted. He was busy with applications to other law schools when he received a phone call. The fact that he was a homicide detective seemed to fascinate the law department at Harvard. He was granted admission. The women in his life had come as just as much a surprise. He never looked for one of them. Each just seemed to show up. He didn't come to Paris looking for a Jill, but there she was. His success as a homicide detective often came from a stray piece of information that showed up on his desk one day. He had a lot of faith in good things and the inability to plan for them.

So he wasn't the least bit surprised that afternoon when he found an apartment.

After browsing for music and books, and after lunch at a sidewalk café, he wandered the maze of streets that stretched to the west of his hotel. He found lots of fascinating shops, some featuring specialized furniture, others expensive works of art, and more that catered to clothing for both men and women. This was Paris, and this was a popular section of town with both the locals and the tourists.

He was walking down one narrow street when he noticed a set of large, wooden doors that stood open. He had seen ones like these a number of times during his walk. He wasn't sure what was behind them. Each set of doors was wide, perhaps sixteen feet, and each had a normal-sized door in one of the double doors. He stopped to peek behind the open doors. What he saw was a courtyard, and then he understood. The courtyards belonged to one or more private homes in the center of the city. The double doors were opened for the owners to drive their cars in.

He stepped in a few paces to get a better look. This was apparently one home, built in a horseshoe around the small courtyard. The right side of the horseshoe was actually a double garage. Grant was surprised when a man stepped from behind one of the open garage doors and stopped in front of him.

"Oui, est-ce que je peux vous aider?"

The question was not meant to be friendly, Grant could tell from the tone, even if it was asked in French. The man appeared to be in his mid-forties. He wasn't very big, but he was trim and muscular, this was evident even though he was wearing an expensive three-piece suit. Grant thought that women would find him handsome, but he had a hard set to his eyes and to his jaw, so that even if he smiled no one would be sure if it was a friendly smile. Simply by his stance, Grant decided the man was confident, and he was used to getting what he wanted. He leaned a little forward, aggressively, and his hands were slightly curved-in, ready for action.

Grant stepped back and smiled. He wasn't interested in pushing the man's buttons. In his barely adequate French, he tried to explain to the man that he was simply curious about what was behind these doors. He had seen several sets, but these were the first he'd seen open.

He didn't wince or smile, as some Frenchmen did when Grant tried his limited language skills. He simply asked, "American?"

"Yes," Grant said.

The man slipped into English. His French accent was still strong, but he spoke English with ease. "As you can see, it opens onto a courtyard. This is my home. It is *not* a tourist attraction."

"I apologize," Grant said. "I'm just trying to become more familiar with my neighborhood."

"You're not a tourist?" the man asked.

"I work in Paris, but I've only been here a little over a week. I guess that still makes me a tourist of sorts."

"Where are you working?"

Grant doubted if the man would understand since even most Americans didn't know about his job, but he gave a brief description of his work.

"The Legat Office? Are you an FBI agent?"

Now Grant was curious. Since few Americans would make the connection between the Legat Office and the FBI, he wanted to know how this Frenchman had made it. "I'm a researcher, or in other words, a field representative, but I'm not an agent. How do you know about the Legat Office?"

The man ignored the question. "Are you a lawyer?"

"Actually I am, but I'm not in practice."

"The school?"

"Harvard."

The man's body language changed. His hands relaxed and he stood up straight. "You have a law degree from Harvard and you're a bureaucrat? You must really have wanted to work in Paris."

"I was a homicide detective before that. I wanted a break."

"Come in and let me shut the gates. I just came back from the country. I have work to prepare for Monday." When they stepped into the courtyard, the man swung the two big doors to the gate closed and latched them firmly from the inside. He then checked to see if the small door was locked, which it was. Having done that, he walked to the double doors that opened into one of the garage bays. An expensive Mercedes was parked inside and the trunk was open. He lifted a briefcase and a suitcase from the trunk, shut it, then closed and locked the doors to the garage.

Having done all of that without a word, he finally turned back to Grant and asked, "What is your name?"

Grant told him.

"Where are you living in Paris?"

Grant told him that as well.

He was silent for a long time, his stare seeming to cut through Grant. Finally he asked, "A hotel? Isn't that expensive?"

"It's not a very good hotel," Grant said.

"You're staying there while you are looking for a place?"

"Actually I haven't been looking for a place."

The man nodded his head over his right shoulder. "That row of windows above the garage is the front room of an apartment. It's not a large apartment; it has only a living room, a bedroom, a bath and a small kitchen. If you check out, I will rent it to you for a thousand American a month."

"And why would you do that?" Grant asked.

"I had a graduate student living there who was going to the Sorbonne. He just finished. The place is empty, I'm gone a lot, and I like to have someone around to keep an eye on the place."

"A thousand dollars seems cheap for a place in this part of Paris."

"I'm a lawyer," he said. "I'm reducing the rent because I plan to consult with you about American law."

"I may not be able to help you a lot. My focus was on criminal law."

"Even better."

Now Grant needed to know some things. The last thing he wanted to do was get tied up with a lawyer who represented a criminal element. "Just exactly who is it you represent?"

The man smiled. "I don't think we will have a conflict of interests here. I represent Frenchmen doing business in America and in trouble with the U.S. tax codes. If my clients are found guilty, they pay penalties; they don't usually go to jail."

"How often are they found guilty?" Grant asked.

"I have a chateau in the south of France, apartments in London and in New York, and a townhouse in Washington, D.C.; with a mistress in each place. I don't lose often." He gestured to the room again. "The apartment is furnished, it has a television connected to a satellite dish, but you have no place for a car. The house does not come with a mistress. Help me carry my bags inside and have a drink while I make a few calls."

An hour later Grant was walking the few blocks back to his hotel, wondering how he was going to break the news to the owner that he would be leaving after all.

His new landlord's name was Gilles Gide. Grant had been left with a glass of wine in the opulent living room of the townhouse while Gide had made a few phone calls. When he returned a half an hour later, he tossed keys to the apartment to Grant and said, "The apartment has a phone. I'll give you a bill for the utilities at the end of each month, which I will expect you to pay with the rent."

Grant was always suspicious of something that was too easy. He wanted to know the specifics of the rental, or was it a lease? Gide had a short list of responsibilities for Grant. They included checking the security of the house each night before he went to bed, monitoring the cleaning lady when she came in once a week while he was away, taking important calls and having them transferred to a number Gide would leave behind when he traveled, and running errands if necessary. Grant was also to make himself available for consultation on occasion, should a case Gide was handling warrant it.

In exchange, Grant was getting a handsome apartment in the middle of Paris for a small part of what it was worth.

Grant tossed the keys back to Gide and said, "I may not be a practicing lawyer, but I have passed the bar. I suspect you will cover the cost of the apartment through consultation fees you don't have to pay. I don't see this as being a particularly good deal for me, and, besides, I already have a place to live."

The keys came flying back to him. "Name your terms."

"I'll pay you eight hundred a month and you pick up the utilities."

The man thought for only a moment. "Done, but I won't pay your long distance phone bills."

"Done."

Grant felt a little bit guilty after he saw the apartment. A door next to the garage led to an enclosed flight of stairs wedged between the apartment and the house. A door opened into the kitchen of the apartment on the top landing. The apartment had only three rooms. The kitchen, a dining room, and the living room formed an L. The kitchen wasn't very big but it was equipped with modern appliances, including a microwave. At the corner of the L was a dining table with four chairs. The living room stretched across the rest of the front of the apartment, well lighted with six, tall, arched windows. A large, overstuffed sofa dominated the area under the windows, and two matching chairs with ottomans flanked each side of a large fireplace, outfitted with a gas firebox. In one corner of the room, next to a door that Grant guessed led to the bedroom, was a large-screen television set, easily visible from the sofa.

The décor was pleasant. Lots of wood, and a coffee table, end tables, and a writing desk on the wall between two more arched windows that looked down on the street below.

The bedroom was filled with an antique bedroom set made from hand-carved cherry wood, including a bed, a dresser, a side table, and a vanity topped with marble. The headboard and mirror stood at least eight feet tall, appropriate to a room with a twelve-foot ceiling.

Off the bedroom was a bathroom with a walk-in shower and a large spa tub. Behind folding doors was the one thing that made the apartment a prize for Grant, a hidden, stacked washer and dryer combination. Connected to the bathroom was a small dressing area with a huge antique armoire that dominated the space.

Gilles had asked when he would be moving in. Grant was tempted to say immediately, but he explained that he had a date that night, a trip to Pigalle for the first time with a co-worker, so he would be moving in the next day. "It won't take much packing," he said. "I travel light."

Again Gilles disappeared into the house, and then he came back a few minutes later with a slip of paper. "I've made arrangements for you to take in a dinner and a show at le Crazy Horse Saloon," he said. "My treat. The manager owes me a favor. On the key ring is one for the door in the gate. I have the lock on your apartment wired so that when you lock it on the inside a light in the security panel in my house tells me that you are home, and when you lock it from the outside, another tells me you are gone. Please keep the door locked. I'm not going to be keeping tabs on you, but I do like to know when I'm alone and when I am not.

"You're free to have guests. The walls in these old houses are thick, and as long as you do not blast your television or your stereo, your noise won't bother me. I do need quiet to concentrate. On Monday I will have some paperwork drawn up that will put all of this into writing. As one lawyer to another, I'm sure I don't have to tell you to read it before you sign it."

Grant was in a great mood when he arrived back at his hotel, pleased with his good fortune. He wasn't a fool, though; he didn't turn into the hotel. Instead he entered his office building. He'd heard the expression not to look a gift horse in the mouth, but he had thought the first time he heard it how different things might have been if someone had looked the Trojan Horse in the mouth.

Jill was gone when he entered the office. He would have to tell her about the apartment over dinner. He's heard of this Crazy Horse place, thinking it was pretty notorious. Should be an interesting night.

He made himself comfortable at his desk, and then he logged onto the computer. Within a few minutes he was reading everything he could find about Gilles Gide.

Grant was so focused on finding out about Gide he paid no attention to the man who was window shopping at a store at the end of his street. He paid attention to Grant, though. He watched him walk down the street in the reflection of the glass, expecting him to enter his hotel. He was mildly surprised to see Grant turn into the office building instead.

It did not matter. He knew where to find Grant. Finding him was important after the phone call this morning. His client was a bit panicky, unusual for him. He made it clear during the call that Grant Reynolds was beginning to nose around in too many of the right places. The Assassin was to be prepared. Reynolds would need to be eliminated if he got any closer.

NINETEEN

The strippers who delighted in removing their G-strings and tossing them into the audience was about what he had expected from le Crazy Horse Saloon. But to make matters worse, Gide had provided them with a ringside table so there was no way he could discreetly miss the action. Nude women and dinner were not the best combination, he thought, at least when you're on a date.

He was concerned about what Jill would think, but he was relieved when she took it all in with a certain glee, the strippers and the vaudeville skits in between. Jill knew this was a Parisian tourist stop, and took it in with amusement. But she did say once during the evening, "If this were not Paris, this would be totally inappropriate." Inappropriate or not, she had fun.

If it hadn't been for the research that Grant had done on Gilles Gide, he would have been suspicious. When they arrived at the club and Grant had given his name, the two of them were ushered to a reserved table next to the stage. When it came time to pay, the bill was whisked away, but not before Grant had seen the total. With drinks and dinner, the tab had come close to $400 U.S. dollars. Grant did leave an appropriate tip, which he noted would have been enough money alone for the two of them to have a pleasant evening in a less expensive part of Paris.

Grant did not doubt for a minute that Gide could afford

the generous gesture, nor did he doubt that Gide had his reasons for being so generous. Gide was everything he said he was, and much, much more. He was senior partner in a law firm with over a hundred lawyers. The firm specialized in representing French nationals in foreign courts. The success of the firm had made Gide both a wealthy and a powerful man, one who was often asked to serve his government as a consultant, a representative, or even a high-profile committee member. Grant learned from James Smith that Gide's name was on a short list of potential future presidents of France.

Grant also learned that Gide had been married, had been caught up in an unpleasant divorce, and had spent a small fortune to be free of the wife. He contented himself with his work, his various homes, and the women he had encamped in each spot except for the Paris house.

Smith's only warning to Grant about mixing with someone as powerful as Gide was to expect to be used. That, and Smith doubted that the embassy would be excited to know of his relation with the French lawyer. Someone as lowly as Grant wasn't expected to rub elbows with the powerful. The ambassador was expected to do that.

Grant had to agree that the warning was a good one, but later that evening when he opened the door to the apartment and led Jill into it for the first time, he threw caution to the wind. He, like Gide, appreciated the house for its location, its style, and its isolation.

Jill was impressed, too. She could not believe his good fortune, and, to keep questions from being raised, he didn't tell her how much he was paying for the place.

"You can't be more than a few blocks from work, perfectly located between Notre Dame and the Musée d'Orsay. A tourist would be delighted to find a hotel available in this area, but to find an apartment, especially one that's part of a private home ..." She let that trail off. "By the way, who owns the house?"

He was tempted to lie simply because he knew Gide's name might cause complications, but he also knew that once he gave the embassy his new address, the security staff there would check it out and Gide's name would come up. He said, "A lawyer by the name of Gilles Gide."

Jill slowly sank down in one of the overstuffed chairs by the fireplace and said, "Are you an idiot?"

"Not according to Harvard Law School," he said.

"Do you know who Gide is?"

"Wasn't he a French writer?"

"Don't be a smartass with me. He's one of the most powerful men in Paris, and he's pretty high up on the power scale in France. Christ, he's had dinner in the White House. What are you doing messing around with him?"

"Renting."

"The embassy will shit bricks. The ambassador will have a stroke. Have you thought about why Gide would rent this place to you?"

"I had a top secret, code-word security clearance in military intelligence, I'm a former cop, and I'm a lawyer. Maybe he thinks I'm a good risk for a renter. I probably won't book in the middle of the night and take the furniture with me."

"Gide doesn't need the rent money. If you're here it's because he has a use for you."

"Gide represents French nationals in American courts. He likes the idea of an American lawyer living nearby with whom he can consult."

"I hope that's all it is," she said, "but even that could be considered a conflict of interest. You'll hear from the embassy on this one, and I wouldn't be surprised if they told you to move out." She got up and made a quick tour of the apartment, checking out the bedroom and bathroom and then ending up in the kitchen. When she was done, she did add, "Of course if they do force you to move out, could you talk to Gide and see if I could have the place?"

"I don't think that will happen. This is his retreat from women."

She came to him. "Is this going to be your retreat from women, too?"

He shrugged. "So far I haven't had to fight them off."

She moved into his arms and kissed him on the lips. When she pulled back, she whispered, "I've had too much to drink and I'm not responsible for my actions, so take me to bed before I change my mind."

One thing that Grant had learned in his life was that the complications from saying no to an attractive woman who invited him to bed were far worse than the complications from going to bed would be. Besides, he told himself, he'd had too much to drink and he wasn't responsible for his actions.

They both remained irresponsible until the darkest hours of the night.

In the morning, when he woke to find Jill's naked body still in bed with him, the same phrase ran over and over again in his head: peaches and cream. That described her, from the paleness of her skin to blushes that highlighted it, that little tuff of hair, the nipples, the color of her cheeks when she turned passionate. And she could turn passionate.

He expected awkwardness and embarrassment when Jill woke, but he was more than pleased when it didn't happen. She rolled over and curled up in his arm with her head on his chest. "Thanks," she said. "It would be an understatement to say I needed that."

"A gross understatement," he said.

He could feel her face on his chest break into a smile. "I thought I sensed a little urgency on your part as well," she said, poking him gently in the ribs.

"It had been awhile," he said.

"I hope that's because you're selective," she said.

"Selective to the point of being exclusive."

"You know how to say all the right things to a woman."

"It's easy when it's the right woman."

They took their time getting out of bed. After another round of lovemaking, he slipped out to get them food. It was afternoon before they showered and dressed. She had to get back to her apartment. Both had turned off their cell phones, so there was no telling what might have happened while they were out of touch with the embassy.

He walked her to the gate and kissed her goodbye before letting her out. The last thing she said was, "Don't let them force you to move."

He knew exactly what she meant. This was a perfect spot to hide from prying eyes. He now knew why Gide preferred it.

He did not get back to the hotel until late in the afternoon. The man was on the street again, this time at a different shop window, and he was waiting, a bit impatiently now, for Grant to return. Again Grant did not notice him.

The man was content that his information about Reynolds' habits was accurate and moved on to another store window before slowly drifting off.

The manager wasn't as devastated as Grant imagined he would be. By, in essence, leasing Grant a room, he had been pushing French laws a bit. Grant's departure would make his life a little less complicated. The fact that Grant told him to keep the rent for the rest of the month for his inconvenience helped too.

Grant was packed within an hour. It took him only three trips to carry his possessions to the apartment. An hour later he was unpacked and settled in.

About nine in the evening he heard footsteps on the stairwell followed by a tap on his door. When he opened the door, Gide stood on the landing with a decanter in one hand—of what turned out to be brandy—and two glasses in the other hand. "I thought we might celebrate your moving in."

Even though the evening was mild and the fire not turned on, the two moved to the chairs in front of the fireplace and made themselves comfortable after Gide poured them drinks. "You won't find a brandy better than this," he said.

The brandy was good, but Grant didn't have enough experience drinking it to know if it was as good as Gide said it was. "This is going to take a little time to get used to. I haven't had this much space in some time."

"The house is perhaps twenty times larger than this, and I seem to use every room. I have an office for myself, an office for my secretary should I choose to work at home, a conference room, a law library, a library, a pool room ... I like the idea of a room for every mood."

"But no woman to share it with," Grant said.

"If I had a woman, I wouldn't have the space. The woman would occupy it all. By the way, I did notice your visitor this afternoon. You have good taste."

Grant laughed. "Yes I do."

"Do you work together?"

"We do."

"As a lawyer to a lawyer, let me advise you to go cautiously. I don't recommend you date women in the workplace, although I do it all the time."

The memory of last night flashed through Grant's mind. "I think it's a little too late for that."

Gide added more brandy to each glass and then settled back again. "Have you ever been married?"

"No," Grant said.

"Good. I can use you to help me stay single, another duty."

"About the duties," Grant said. "I can't get caught up in a conflict of interest, and my focus in law school was on criminal law, not tax laws. In addition, I don't carry with me a set of law books."

"Are you already trying to shirk your duties?"

"Not at all. I just don't want to be accused of misrepresentation."

"You need not worry. I don't want a conflict of interest any more than you do. As I am sure you have found out by now, I am a political creature. My former wife was able to take advantage of that in our divorce settlement.

"As far as the work with the law is concerned, I suspect what I need more than anything is someone who can explain to me what the English means. Law books are the same in any language: almost incomprehensible. I speak English fairly well, but reading law books in English can be an arduous task for me. When I'm working at home, I don't want to have my assistants running in and out. I work at home to get away from them."

"And you don't think you will tire of me?" Grant asked.

"You fascinate me," he said. "You have an unusual collection of skills. I'm drawn to useful people."

"Hopefully it will be mutual," Grant said, seeing an opportunity to turn the tables on Gide. "Perhaps you can help."

Gide, a true Frenchman, shrugged with both corners of his mouth turned down, a classic gesture. "Perhaps."

Grant looked off in the distance. He didn't want Gide to know how important any information about this could be to him. "Have you ever heard of a company by the name of Euro-Arts?"

The same exaggerated expression again. "This is a company quite well known among my circle of acquaintances."

Continuing to stare, this time into a fire that was not burning, Grant asked, "What can you tell me about it?"

Gide rested his chin on his left hand while he gave the question some thought. After a sip of brandy, he said, "This is a multi-service company for the serious art collector. The company discreetly advertises works of arts, negotiates sales between private parties, provides insurance for collections, arranges secure transportation for works of arts, and invests in new, young artists with potential."

"For a company that does so much, I find it to be a difficult firm to contact," Grant said.

"The clientele is exclusive. I doubt that you have the kind of income that would interest Euro-Arts, and I can guarantee the company will honor the privacy of its clients."

"Have you dealt with the company?"

"As a client?" Guide asked. And then he answered his own question. "No. I leave the decorations, including the works of arts, to professional decorators. This house I bought as you see it, complete with the furnishings, which included the art. Although I understand that some of the paintings in the main house have a little value, most do not. The owner, by the way, died having outlived his heirs. The purchase price of the house went to his favorite charities. He was a bishop—retired, if bishops do such things."

"Have you represented clients who were dealing with Euro-Arts?"

"Obviously I can't betray who, but, yes, I have. Contractual things."

"Have you heard anything that would suggest that Euro-Arts is doing something illegal?" This time Grant turned to look at Gide's face. He wanted to see the man's reaction to the question. He was surprised when Gide laughed.

"Some rather well-known people would have serious heart flutters if that were true. To answer your question, though, no, I haven't heard any proof of Euro-Arts doing anything illegal."

Grant lifted his glass to his lips to hide his smile. He noted the way that Gide had worded the response. No proof. He did not say that he hadn't heard of anything illegal. Grant decided not to push it now. He was sure that he was on to something, but he wasn't sure yet what it was.

Gide finished his drink and then rose from the chair. "I need to get back to my work," he said. "Would you mind if we did this a few times a week: get together for a nightcap? It's not often that I get to make the acquaintance of someone new, especially someone who has been in military intelligence, has been a homicide detective, and who has a law degree from Harvard but chooses not to practice law."

Grant might have added that it wasn't often that he got to hobnob with the French elite, but he said instead, "I'd enjoy that. I hope that we can be mutually helpful to each other."

Gide left the decanter of brandy, now half full, and walked to the door. "I never liked this door," he said. "The idea of entering a house through the kitchen seems all wrong."

"For the rent I'm paying," Grant said, "I can suffer the door in the wrong place."

Gide shook his hand and said, "Goodnight then."

As he watched the Frenchman walk down the steps,

Grant had two thoughts. Even successful, powerful, and wealthy men must get lonely sometimes. Gide, tonight, seemed like a lonely man, but that was to be expected. The divorce was still fresh, and he hadn't been alone in Paris for that long.

The second thing that caught his attention was that Gide knew about his military service. He hadn't talked about it, so both he and Gide had done their homework.

As he turned off the light to the stairwell and locked himself in the apartment, he played with one more idea. Gide knew more about Euro-Arts than he was willing to share. Grant would have to work on him to get the rest, but carefully. He liked the idea of having Gide as a friend.

He put the decanter on the mantel over the fireplace and took the glasses to the kitchen sink to be washed in the morning. As he walked back through the apartment, turning off lights as he went, he, too, felt the sudden chill of loneliness. In the bedroom, he propped up pillows against the headboard and made himself comfortable on the bed. He picked up his cell phone from the lamp table next to the bed and stared at it for a moment. He then turned it on, found the name he was looking for, and pushed the speed dial button. He hoped that Jill had not gone to bed yet.

TWENTY

They were lucky that Dale Bailey wasn't in the office on Monday morning. He would have known that they had slept together. The two of them were awkward with each other. Grant wasn't sure if they should hug when they met in the office, or whether they should pretend that nothing extraordinary had taken place. It didn't help that Jill was just as indecisive.

After ten minutes of avoiding eye contact through strained conversations, Jill was the one finally to confront the issue. "We're acting like a couple of teenagers," she said, "not sure if they have done something naughty or not."

He was glad she broke the ice on the subject. He was starting to wonder if he had made a huge mistake. "This is Paris," he said. "Nothing is naughty."

"Maybe not naughty, but not necessarily wise," she said. "Look, I absolutely enjoyed myself. All of it, if there's any doubt in your mind. I'd like to do it again, but I don't want it to interfere with our work."

"Suggestions?"

"Weekends. We spend Saturdays, Saturday nights together. It's not like we don't see each other during the week."

He liked that. It gave them some time together, and it gave them some time alone. And it drew a distinct line between work and play. "I like the idea," he said.

"Good," she said. "Now let me go get us some good coffee, and then let's start this day over again." She picked up her purse and headed out the door.

She was gone no more than a few minutes when the phone rang. Grant answered the call and found Linda Ebenhart on the other end of the line. "You're up early," he said.

"I just got back from my jog. I thought I might hear from you this weekend."

Cautiously, relaxed again, he said, "I appreciate the thought. On the other hand, I think you understand that you represent a client who is part of a murder investigation. I think it would be conflict of interest if we saw each other until something is resolved here."

"I thought we had this resolved. You really have no reason to bother Walter. He has assured you that this has nothing to do with him."

"I hope I didn't give you that idea. Too much is still not clear about Tiffany's murder. I will want to talk to Walter at some time, but I do respect his need for time to work through his grief." This, he thought to himself, was what it meant to be a diplomat.

"Is there any chance we could have lunch today and talk about this?"

"Mondays are busy," he said, which he had been told by Jill was true, although this Monday was the exception because apparently Americans had managed to stay out of trouble over the weekend.

"Later in the week?"

Later in the week, depending on what they managed to find out in the next couple of days, might be a good idea. He might have more questions he wanted answered by then. "I'll have time on Thursday, I think," he said.

"That long?" She sounded disappointed.

"If I can move it up, I'll give you a call," he said.

"I would like to spend some time with you while I'm in Paris," she said. "We didn't part under the best of circumstances."

"I think it was called graduation."

"You know what I mean. My parents didn't embrace you with open arms, and you were upset by it."

"I didn't think you noticed," he said.

"I noticed. I was disappointed in you. All along I thought it was about you and me, and then I find out that in your mind my parents became part of the mix."

He would have said exactly the same thing to her. He had neatly packed away the relationship between them and stored it in a "Do Not Open" container, and now here she was telling him he had gotten it all wrong. With Jill in the picture, he was sure he did not want to go backward. The relationship between him and Linda was history, and this was business. "Someday maybe we can talk about that, but for now I can't separate Linda the lawyer from my job as Grant the investigator."

"I understand that. But I'm taking it as a promise that we will talk about it before I leave Paris."

"Fair enough," he said.

After they said goodbye, he felt relieved that the conversation had ended before Jill returned. He was not a man to play one woman off another, nor was he one who would want a woman to think he was.

He called the embassy and notified them of his change of address. He was relieved when the secretary took down the information without suggesting that he needed to talk to someone higher up. As he hung up the phone, Jill returned with the coffee.

This time, with issues settled between them, they were able to get down to work. Jill drank her coffee quickly because she planned to return to the Louvre to talk to the assistant director about the paintings Sutherlin purchased. She had promised to take the woman to lunch, so Jill said not to expect her back before mid-afternoon.

Grant spent the morning writing reports. Even if nothing happened, reports had to be made and when something did happen, even if it was resolved, follow-up reports needed to be written. By being out of the office so much, Dale had neatly left the report writing to Jill and himself. Clever bastard, Grant thought.

Shortly after returning from lunch, Grant received a phone call from the "clever bastard."

"Jill's out," Grant said when he recognized Dale's voice.

"I didn't call to talk to Jill," he said.

"What can I help you with, Dale?"

"What the hell are you doing?"

"Writing reports."

"Don't be a smartass. I want to know what you're doing moving in with Gilles Gide."

"Smartass" seemed to be a popular word used in connection with myself, he thought. And so much for his move going unnoticed. "I'm renting an apartment from Mr. Gide. I'm certainly not living with him."

"Gide's way out of your league. You want nothing to do with him."

"I'm not having a whole lot to do with him, other than renting an apartment from him. I will be keeping an eye on his property when he's gone, and I have volunteered to explain the meaning of incomprehensible passages in American law books, but I'm not exactly an employee of his."

"Why in the hell would you be telling him something about the law? The man is, for Christ's sake, a hell of a lawyer."

"Dale, I do have a law degree from Harvard."

Dead silence. Grant wondered just what Dale was thinking. Was he thinking that Grant was rubbing his nose with his law degree, or had Dale forgotten, or did he think this was irrelevant? Finally, Dale said, "So?"

"It's a lawyer to lawyer thing—" he said.

Dale cut him off. "And I wouldn't understand."

"Are you telling me to give up the apartment?"

"Yes I am."

"Thanks for sharing. Is there anything else you'd like to talk about?"

"If I have anything else, I'll discuss it with Jill. For you, I have just one more piece of advice: you can be replaced."

"We can all be replaced," Grant said, just before Dale clicked off the phone. Or maybe he threw it against a wall, Grant thought.

A half hour later the phone rang again, and this time it was the ambassador. Grant had yet to spend time with the ambassador, but he did his homework before taking the job in Paris. He knew the ambassador was a kindly man, a self-made multimillionaire, and a party loyalist. He had raised a considerable amount of money to help get the current President elected, and he was given credit for carrying his home state for the president in the last election. His reward was to be made ambassador to France, even though he spoke only a few words of French and had no diplomatic experience. In his favor, Grant thought, was that most ambassadors did not speak the language of the country they were in, and most had no diplomatic experience. Could he be any worse than the next guy? Grant wondered.

"Grant," he said, "I'm sorry we haven't had a chance to talk, but I'm certainly hearing a lot about you."

How ominous could that be? "I believe you're calling about Gilles Gide," he said.

"I, uh, well, yes ..." was the best the ambassador could do. Too much diplomacy, Grant thought. The old man couldn't handle straight talk.

"I'm a lawyer, sir. I understand conflict of interest. I don't have one. In fact, I see several advantages to living at Gide's Paris home. I think he will be an invaluable source of information for me. I also think having me there might open up an informal line of communication with a powerful man who has many important contacts. And, simply, it's a nice apartment with a reasonable rent and a wonderful location. He likes the idea of someone being able to watch his place while he's gone, he likes the idea of renting the apartment to a lawyer, and he particularly likes the idea it is an American lawyer, since so much of his work involves America." He wasn't about to let the ambassador get a word in. "I think the embassy would see my contact with Gide as a valuable resource, not an issue of concern."

"You do make a strong case."

"Like I said, I'm a lawyer."

"For the time being, stay where you are. I will, of course, need to confer with Washington, but I don't see any harm with you living there for now."

"Thank you, sir. I certainly couldn't afford the rent if it were not for my living allowance." He threw that in as an afterthought. He wanted to make it clear that Gide wasn't giving him a gift, even though the low rent could easily be seen that way.

"By the way," the ambassador added, "I've heard good things about you. Some important people tell me you are doing a good job. Keep it up."

"Thank you, sir."

"You'll need to walk on eggs with Walter Sutherlin. He's not a man whose feathers we want to ruffle."

No cliché is too good for the ambassador. "I'm trying

my best to be diplomatic," he said, even with a straight face.

"Perfect. Keep up the good work."

After he hung up, Grant said to the empty office, "What you folks don't know is that I've been playing this game for a long time. In the past it wasn't the ambassador who called, it was the police chief, or the mayor, or some other political creature who told me to walk softly. I didn't listen to them, either."

He had finished his ranting by the time Jill returned from her lunch. They moved to the conference table so they could sit next to each other and share the fruits of their day so far.

He filled her in on his phone calls, including the one from Linda. To her credit, she treated the three as being equally important. Neither the call from Linda nor the call from Dale concerned her, but she had never received a personal call from the ambassador, which might indicate to Grant that the folks at the top were concerned. And, if they were concerned, that meant some folks even higher up in the States were concerned. She thought the ambassador's advice to walk softly wasn't a bad suggestion.

As for her lunch with the assistant director, she couldn't honestly say if she had learned anything of value. "Basically, what she told me about Walter's collection was that he had some good pieces, a few even important ones, but they were the kinds of paintings that they would use at the museum to frame a much more famous painting."

"What exactly does that mean?" he asked.

"She explained that although the Louvre had thousands of masterpieces in one form of art or another, the public isn't particularly well-educated when it comes to art. Because of that, the visitors really only recognize a few, comparatively, masterpieces. In order for the viewers to truly enjoy these masterpieces, the museum surrounds them with lesser works so the uninitiated can see clearly why a particular piece is a masterpiece."

"So, either Walter satisfies his collector urge with lesser works, or he has some more important pieces we don't know about."

She briefly rested her head on his shoulder and said, "You smell good."

"Careful, or you're going to make the weekend too, too far away."

"Sorry." She pulled her head away. "Back to business. If Walter has some major pieces, he didn't get them from Euro-Arts, and I haven't run across any other record of them. As much as I am less than thrilled by the idea of you having dinner with Linda again, I suggest when you do, you ask her about Walter's collection."

"That's a good idea," he said. "What else have we got on our agenda today?"

"Did you get the reports done?"

"Every one, and I faxed them to the embassy."

"And we haven't had any other calls?"

"Not a one."

"Then we call the embassy and tell them to forward our calls to our cell phones, and then we take comp time."

"Comp time?"

"You may not have accumulated much yet, but you will, and I have. I say we take a couple of hours off and enjoy the sunshine."

They sat there for a moment, shoulder to shoulder, slouching in their chairs, and then they both turned to look at the other, their eyes locked in mutual admiration. "Why don't we spend that comp time in my bed?" he asked.

"What about our agreement?"

"We'll start that when Dale gets back."

She gave it some thought, and then she jumped to her feet and grabbed his hand to tug him to his feet. "Let's go," she said.

In that instant he saw the girl in her, and he liked it a lot.

A half hour later, after they'd made the call to the embassy and locked up the office, the Assassin was once again wandering the side street nearby, pretending to window shop, but actually seeing what he could see in the reflection of the windows. After an hour of meandering without catching sight of Reynolds, he drifted off. If he couldn't find the man now, he knew when and where he would be able to find him later.

TWENTY-ONE

He quietly made his way to the landing at the top of the stairs.

He put his ear to the door and listened. Nothing. He was in no hurry. This was the deep of the night, a time so still that even Paris seemed to be deserted. Unlike any other city in the world, many people in Paris gave up new locks for the quaint look of the old. He was an expert at circumventing old locks and easily opened this one. Again he put his ear to the door and listened. Still nothing. He let himself in.

He had unscrewed the light bulb at the top of the landing. He didn't want a sudden flood of light to awaken his victim. Inside, he leaned his back against the door and listened again.

Reynolds was a quiet sleeper. He could just barely make out the quiet, even breathing of the man in his bed. He took his time working his way to the bed. Reynolds was a former policeman. He might have a gun. He was certainly trained in self-defense. He did not want the man to waken.

When he finally stood beside the bed, he realized how easy it would be. The man slept on his side with his back to the Assassin. Enough light came from the window to illuminate his outline. The Assassin eased from his pocket the automatic with the silencer. The gun would make little noise. Getting out unnoticed was as important as getting in unheard.

He slid the barrel of the silencer to the base of Reynolds' skull. The sense of power that always surged in him at this precise moment, surged one more time. In an instant he would take a life. What gave him the most pleasure was the thought that the man would never know what happened. One moment he would be alive; the next moment he would be dead. No drama. No passionate slide from life to death. No begging for mercy. No pleading for more life. No last second attempt at peace with God. Lights on; lights off. Pulling the trigger was no more significant than the flip of a switch. And he had the power to do it.

The puff from the gun caused only a slight change in the man. His breathing faltered. The second puff seemed to make the man sink deeper into the mattress. The awkward reach across the body to insert the silencer in the mouth and the final puff put the man into a permanent sleep.

He left as quietly as he'd come. He knew the danger was not over. He had to make it down the stairs. He had to step back outside. He never knew what to expect right after a kill, and for him that was his favorite time. He loved the danger.

Tonight, as was almost always the case, nothing happened. He was back on the street. No lights came on. No shouts were heard from above. Nothing. He kept to the shadows until he made his way back to the boulevard. Instead of walking along the street and attracting attention to himself, he took steps down to the quay along the Seine. He might have a problem with the bums that slept under the bridges at night, but he wasn't concerned. He still had the gun, and he would not drop it in the Seine until he was ready to take another set of stairs up to a bridge where he would cross back into his part of town.

Twenty minutes later he was entering his apartment building. The gun was gone. He had stepped over several derelicts sleeping under a bridge, but none had awakened. No one had been on the streets to see him. Not even a police car had passed.

Once again he had been an angel of death, swooping in to snuff out a life and swooping back out again unseen. He felt both an incredible sense of joy and an incredible sense of power.

TWENTY-TWO

Jill's phone rang at five-thirty, early even for her. It was Dale. "We think someone's tried to kill Grant."

If she hadn't been awake before, she was now. "What are you saying?"

"The embassy got a call. A man in Grant's room has been shot. The body hasn't been officially identified yet. I need you to get over there."

She didn't even allow him to finish the call. She brushed her teeth and hair, threw on sweatpants and shirt, slipped on tennis shoes, grabbed her purse, and headed outside. She flagged down a cab.

She stood outside the large gate, confused. The street was silent. No police cars. No cops. She moved to the door in the gate and pushed the buzzer. She kept pushing it, a little more frantically as time when on, until finally the door opened a fraction. A woman peeked through the narrow gap.

"Who are you?" Jill demanded.

"I'm the housekeeper."

"Are the police here?"

The woman gave her a very strange look, and then she slammed the door shut. From the other side, she said, "No, but they will be as soon as I call them."

She was confused. Had Dale got it wrong? She thought first to call the embassy, but then the obvious hit her. She pulled her cell phone from her purse and dialed Grant's number. It rang a half a dozen times. Perhaps it hadn't been a mistake. Then she heard Grant's voice.

"This had better be good," he said. "I'm not a pleasant person when I get woken up too early."

"Are you okay?"

"Jill?"

"Are you okay?"

"I'm fine. I would have answered the phone sooner, but I couldn't remember where I left it. This place is only ten times bigger than the last one. It has too many places to set things down."

"Thank God."

"What's wrong?"

"I got a call from Dale. The embassy phoned him and said that you had been shot."

"Who was it who said that the reports of his death were premature?"

"Don't get cerebral on me. I'm at the gate. Come down and let me in. And tell the housekeeper not to call the police."

Grant laughed. "You haven't been partying without me, have you?"

"Get down here," she snapped.

He used the intercom that connected the apartment to the house to let the housekeeper know that the crazed woman at the gate was with him, although he wasn't sure she knew who *he* was.

When he opened the door in the gate, Jill's reaction stunned him. She burst into tears and threw her arms around his neck. He had to pull her arms away to keep from being strangled. When she finally let go of him, she suddenly thumped him on the chest with a fist, and yelled at him, "The next time I get a call that says you've been shot, you'd better be shot."

"Come up to the room," he said.

As they walked to the stairwell, he noticed that the curtains parted in the main house and the housekeeper watched their every move. He hoped she wasn't a great housekeeper or Gide would have to throw him out to keep her happy.

He'd set the coffeemaker the night before. He poured the two of them coffee. The machine only made one cup; they had to share it. When he had her settled into a chair at the dining table, he said, "Tell me one more time what this is all about."

After he heard her story again, he got his cell phone and called the embassy. When he identified himself, he said in response to the secretary, "Yes, I am," followed by, "No, I have not." He listened a few moments and then he ended the call.

"Let me get dressed, and then we have to get back to the office."

"What's going on?" she asked.

"Somebody's been shot."

He couldn't explain anything to her because he knew little himself. The secretary had asked, surprised, if he was alive. She then wanted to know if he had been shot. She could only report that the police had called, and they said they thought that Grant had been shot.

This time there were police, and lots of them. Police cars lined the narrow street below their office. Police officers blocked off both ends of the street and the alley that cut back to la place St-Michel. They were held up at the le quai St-Michel end of the street until Inspector Gerard came down to join them.

"What's going on, Inspector?" Jill asked.

"We've had another murder," he said. He looked at Grant, and he had a slight smile on his face but his eyes were sad. Very sad indeed, Grant thought.

"The Assassin?" he asked.

Gerard nodded. "Three shots to the head."

"Who?" Jill asked.

"An unlucky traveling salesman from Germany who couldn't believe it when he found a room in a hotel at the last moment, especially at the height of tourist season."

"The room?" Grant asked.

"Your former room. He had left an early wake-up call because he had an appointment. When he didn't answer his phone, the manager decided to go to his room. When he didn't answer a knock, the manager let himself in to wake the man. That's when he found the body." Looking apologetic, Gerard added, "The confusion, I'm afraid, is my fault. I associated the room with Grant."

Jill paled. "The killer thought the man was Grant."

Gerard shrugged. "Of course we have a lot to investigate, but that certainly is a possibility. The coincidence of another target being in the same room that Grant had been in ..." He let it trail off. He was sure the victim was meant to be Grant, but he still had to eliminate any other possibility.

"Can I see the crime scene?" Grant asked.

"He was not an American, so I can't let you do that. I'm sorry. I will see that you get all of the information from the crime scene as soon as we have it together."

"Can we go to our office?" Grant asked.

"That will be okay." He said something to the police officers and they stepped aside.

Grant walked away from them. He walked with resolution down the street, into the building, and up to his office. He unlocked the door and turned off the alarm, and then he walked to the windows. He could look across the way and into his former room. He could see the body on the bed, the covers pulled back to expose gray-and-white-striped pajamas. The man might have been asleep except for the stain on the pillow.

When Jill entered the office, Grant was at the safe. He opened it, and then he reached inside to take out one of the guns. He checked the clip on it to see that it was still loaded, and then he took a box of shells from the bottom of the safe.

"We're not authorized to carry weapons," Jill reminded him.

"Then do what you have to do to get the authorization. The Assassin tried to kill me. I am not going to go up against a very dangerous man unarmed. If he tried once, he will try again. Someone wants me dead. Someone may well want you dead."

She wasn't going to back down to him until he said the last bit. She knew as much as Grant did. She had no idea of what either of them could know that might get them killed, but she understood Grant completely. She removed a second gun from the safe and picked up a box of shells. She slipped them into her purse.

"Close the safe," she said. "I'll call the Legal Attaché. He knows how to get the permits for the guns."

Grant had thrown on clothes in his hurry to get to the crime scene. He was wearing jeans and a chambray work shirt. He pulled out the tails of the shirt and unbuttoned it. Underneath he was wearing a dark blue shirt. He made sure a bullet was in the chamber of the automatic and then he flicked the safety off and then on again. Satisfied, he tucked the gun in the back of his pants under his shirt.

"While you call, I have some business to take care of."

Jill looked up from the phone that she'd wedged between the side of her head and her shoulder. "Where are you going?"

"I've got my cell phone. You can reach me if you need to."
He walked out the door.

That was the first time she had seen Grant mad. One
look at him and she knew she wouldn't want to be the one
to make him mad.

Grant wasn't mad. He was fuming. He could think of a
dozen reasons to be irate, the first being that someone had
tried to kill him. The second was that someone ordered the
hit. Both of those were reason enough for him to feel like
killing someone, but he was even madder because he knew
he had been betrayed.

He had already cooled off by the time he reached the
Ile de la Cite. He had learned a long time ago as a rookie
cop that you didn't face the bad guys seeing red. Nothing
good could come of that. People who saw red made stupid
mistakes, the kind that got them killed.

He slipped into the Cathédrale de Notre Dame, feeling
guilty because he was carrying a weapon, and he kneeled
in the back and gave thanks in prayer that he had been
spared, prayed for the soul of the man killed, and asked for
guidance to do the right thing. Before he left the church,
he lit candles for the dead.

He left the church much more in control of his emotions. More than anything that was what he got from
religion, the road to inner peace. He wasn't out to sell it
to anyone else, he felt no absolutes about God or heaven,
but he did know that it worked for him. That alone was the
only important issue.

He walked through the hotel lobby, expecting someone
to try to stop him from going up, but the clerk behind the
desk was the same one who had been on the night he met
Linda in the lobby. The man nodded to him as he walked
toward the elevator, and then he went back to his paperwork.

Grant could feel the anger rise with the elevator. By the time he got off on Linda's floor, he knew he would have trouble keeping it in check. He knocked on her door, a little louder than he needed to. He could see movement behind the peephole in the door, and then the deadbolt turned and the door flew open.

"Grant, you did decide to come," she said.

He walked in without being invited. He noted that she did not have a room but a suite. Double doors led to a bedroom. The living room had a bar and a kitchenette. She shut the door and joined him, the expression on her face telling it all. She knew him well enough to know when he was mad.

"Is something wrong?" she asked.

"I'm sure you reported back to Walter after you talked to me," he said. "Did you talk to anyone else?"

She moved behind the bar, apparently feeling the need to put something between them. "You sound upset," she said.

"Would you please answer my question."

"Please don't forget that I am a lawyer and I represent a client. Whatever has transpired between Walter and myself is protected by lawyer/client privilege."

He walked over to the bar and leaned across its top until his face was no more than a foot from hers. "At the moment I don't give a shit about privilege. In my bed, in the one I have slept in for more than a week, is the body of a poor, unfortunate German salesman who made the mistake of renting my room right after I had vacated it. He now has three bullets in his head, one to the back of the neck, one to the side of the head, and one through the roof of his mouth. He is quite dead, and I have absolutely no doubt that the man who killed him, the same one who killed Tiffany Sutherby, intended to kill me. Right now I'm not in the mood for beating around the bush."

She paled. "What has this got to do with me?" she asked, but he could tell by the look on her face that she suspected it had a lot to do with her.

"I've moved my investigation in only one direction, and that's been toward Walter Sutherlin. Ever since I started he's tried to exert political influence to stop me, then he sent you to try to stop me, and now the man we call the Assassin shows up to try to kill me. I don't think that it's a coincidence that this assault came shortly after my dinner with you."

She looked stricken, but Grant wasn't going to be impressed by anything but the answers to the questions he wanted answered. "Grant, you can't possibly think that I would have something to do with an attempt on your life."

"I'd like to think not," he said, "but I don't believe in these kinds of coincidences."

To her credit, she had not backed away from him. She kept her face a foot from his, and she kept her eyes on his. "Of course I reported back to Walter," she said. "That's part of what he pays me to do."

"What did he say when you did?"

"Nothing. He just listened."

"He didn't ask anything about me?"

"No, but if Walter wanted to know about you, he would. I'm only one of a few thousand people who work for his businesses."

"Did he seem satisfied with what you told him?"

"I don't know. Like I said, he didn't say anything."

"What can you tell me about his art collection?"

She snapped her head back. "What? What on earth does that have to do with anything?"

"Have you seen it?"

"He doesn't show it to everyone, but he does have a small museum in one wing of his mansion. I was given the tour when I first went to work for him."

"Does he have any major pieces?"

She leaned back on the counter. "Grant, we went to the same law school. How many art courses did you have time for?"

"What do you remember about the collection? Can you give me any names of artists?"

She stared at the ceiling, and her mouth took on the near pout he'd found so cute at one time. She scrunched up her nose. He had to look away. She was still a beautiful woman, and he apparently wasn't completely immune to her charms yet. Finally her eyes snapped back to his. "Degas was one."

"What was the painting?"

"Something to do with ballet girls."

"Christ," he said. "A lot of Degas' paintings featured ballet girls."

She threw her hands in the air. "Forgive me for not being an expert."

"Any other names?"

"Chagall."

"Any more?"

"I think maybe a Rembrandt."

"And?"

She let out a blast of air that fluttered her lips. "I'm lucky to remember those," she said. "Most of my parents' friends have art collections featuring impressive artists. After awhile you get bored seeing them."

No trips to the Louvre for Linda. "I'll have more questions."

"You have my phone number," she said.

He reached across the counter and gently brushed a cheek with the tips of his fingers. "I apologize," he said. "Although I knew it couldn't be, I was afraid that you might have betrayed me."

"You know I wouldn't do that," she said. "You haven't got a clue of how much I loved you once."

He was an expert in interrogation. He could tell even when the most accomplished of liars was lying. Linda hadn't lied to him once. Not even with the last statement. "I loved you once, too," he said. He wasn't ready for this conversation. He walked toward the door.

Linda rushed from behind the counter and grabbed an arm to turn him to her. "I won't talk to Walter this time," she said.

"No," he said. "I want you to."

"But if any of this is true, that could put you in more danger."

"I'll take the chance."

She put her arms around him and hugged him tightly in a long embrace. "Is that what I think that is?" she asked.

"It depends on what we're talking about," he said, laughing to hide his embarrassment.

"I'm talking about the hard thing *behind* your back." She laughed too, adding, "I'm glad to see I still have that effect on you."

"Yes, it's a gun."

"Then you think you're still in danger."

"I know the Assassin as well as anyone in police work knows him. I know he's going to be mad when he finds out he got the wrong guy, and I know he's determined not to make the same mistake again. His reputation's taken a hit recently, and I have a feeling that he would do anything to right his listing ship."

"You could stay here with me," she said, "until the danger has passed."

That would be trading one danger for another, he thought. "The danger will pass when we have the Assassin in custody. That isn't going to happen if I'm hiding out here."

"Where can I get in touch with you?" she asked. He gave her a look that suggested that she didn't get it. But she did get it. "That was a stupid question," she added.

"Call the embassy. They'll get a message to me, and I'll call you. In the meantime, if you see me, you see me. Right now I've got to keep my head down." He gently detached himself from her and opened the door. "And call Walter," he said, as he shut the door behind him.

When he walked in the door of the office, he could see the strain on Jill's face. It slowly drained away as he pulled the gun from the back of his pants and stuck it in a drawer before sitting at his desk.

"The Legal Attaché said we were not to carry a weapon, no matter what, until he has talked to the French government. The French don't like armed foreigners on their soil."

"Then they should catch the Assassin. He's the one shooting everyone."

"Where did you go?" she asked.

"I went to see Linda."

An eyebrow shot up. "For ...?"

"Am I the only one who thinks it's funny that the Assassin would try to take me out right after I had dinner with Linda?"

"That's what you get for seeing another woman."

He glanced up in time to see the wry smile on Jill's face. "I failed to see the humor in that at the moment," he said.

"What did Linda have to say?"

"That she reported back to Walter after she talked to me."

"I'm glad she hasn't lost sight of her true purpose for being here."

"Catty this morning, aren't we?"

"I can smell her perfume from here."

He had no clever response for that. "Any calls?"

Jill noted the change of direction to the conversation. "Well, the President hasn't called yet, but just about everyone else has. A call of concern from the ambassador. A call from Dale saying he's coming back. The Legal Attaché responding to my request to be armed. James Smith, who seems to have little birdies who keep him informed of everything involving the Assassin."

"Am I supposed to return any of these calls?"

"The one to James Smith."

He picked up his phone and called Smith. The man seemed to be sitting on his phone, waiting for the call. When he heard it was Grant, he said, "Bloody hell, I'm impressed. You've got the Assassin coming to you."

"Let me assure you, I'm impressed, too. I don't have any information for you yet, because the police have locked me out of this one."

"Don't apologize," Smith said. "I'll get the information before you will. That's not what I'm calling about. I've found out some information about the hat."

"Are we talking about *the* hat?"

"The same one. We've got a half dozen positive ID's, each from a different hit. Our man seems to have a favorite hat."

Grant knew that police work was putting together a lot of little pieces of a puzzle until a picture emerged. He also knew how few pieces they had pertaining to the Assassin. As much as he would like to think otherwise, he doubted that the hat would lead to the killer. But, he also knew that dumb luck played a part as well.

"Can you trace the hat?"

"The hat was modestly popular twenty years ago. It was sold in Europe at exclusive hat shops. The good news is that it was sold in only twenty-five shops total. The bad news is that twenty-two of those shops are now out of business. The good news is that one of those shops is in Paris."

Grant calculated the odds. The Assassin may have bought one of the hats in one of twenty-five stores over twenty years ago. Or, someone may have bought it for him and given it to him as a gift. Or he may have bought it in a thrift shop, or he may have inherited it from a relative, or he may have stolen it. "Do you have the name of the shop?"

"I've got both the name and the address."

Grant wrote down the information. "I'll see what I can do with this."

"Good luck," Smith said. "If anything new comes up from the forensic evidence for this last hit, I'll let you know."

"Thanks." He hung up.

He turned to say something to Jill, but just then the door opened and Gerard came in. Grant wasn't glad to see the inspector. He had a feeling that Gerard was going to get in the way of what Grant needed to do to catch the Assassin.

Gerard didn't waste time getting to the point. "I understand that your government is requesting permission for the two of you to carry weapons. I've asked that permission not be given."

Grant didn't say anything, but Jill was less reserved. "Our lives are in danger and you're not going to let us have the means to protect ourselves?" she asked.

"I will provide you each with twenty-four-hour protection. You will each have a bodyguard. I can't, though, allow you to carry guns. This isn't America."

"And you have no crime in France, and only the good guys carry guns," Jill snapped back.

"Fewer guns, fewer problems," Gerard said, maintaining an air of patience.

"And if we do get caught carrying a gun, what will happen?" Grant asked.

"You'll be arrested, tried, convicted, and either jailed and/or deported."

"Thanks for looking out for us," Jill said.

"You will have the protection of my best people. Please understand that I have to best represent the interests of my country. Americans are not very popular here. If our people found out we were letting Americans carry guns, I'm afraid we'd have a problem more serious than your safety."

"The Assassin has proven himself more clever than dozens of police agencies around the world," Grant reminded him. "You may as well serve us up on a platter to the killer."

"I appreciate your concern for your safety. I am as concerned. Two officers are outside the door now. Each is armed. They have been given orders to escort the two of you wherever you need to go."

Grant scooped his cell phone from his desk, and walked to the door. "Then my fellow gets to go for a walk." To Jill he said, "I'm going to follow up on the information Smith gave me." He lifted a hand to Gerard in a goodbye gesture, but he didn't bother to look at the inspector.

As soon as he closed the door and headed down the stairs, one of the officers, a male, followed after him. A female officer remained behind.

Over his shoulder, Grant said, "We're on our way to l'avenue Montaigne." His bodyguard remained silent and trailed behind Grant by a few paces.

He was on his way to the hat shop Smith mentioned, located in one of the most prestigious shopping districts in Paris. He didn't expect to find out anything, but he needed to get out of the office and away from Gerard, who had disappointed him.

He also needed to put a little distance between Jill and himself. The meeting with Linda had unnerved him. He was sure he'd put his feelings for her behind him, but the second meeting made a mockery of that. By the time he had crossed the Seine, the shuffling of feet reassuring behind him, he had a smile on his face. In a little over a week he'd become involved with a co-worker, something he'd said he wouldn't do again, and he was emotionally stimulated by Linda, something else he'd said he'd never let happen again.

Over his shoulder, he said to the officer behind him, "They weren't kidding when they said Paris is the city of love, were they?"

TWENTY-THREE

He was feeling pleased with himself. He had slipped in and out of the hotel unseen. He had eliminated Mr. Reynolds with little effort, and he had been promised the full amount to eliminate Reynolds' curiosity.

He left his apartment and walked to the elevator. With new money coming in, he thought he might treat himself to a new suit from his favorite *la tailleur.* He had been forced to cut back some these last few years. Suits had been one of the cuts.

He wasn't one to question the motives of the men who hired him. If they felt the need to have someone killed, he was more than happy to do it for a full fee. He tried to stay out of the emotions or the politics involved. He did, though, wonder about killing Reynolds. That might take the heat off for the moment, but the Americans had extensive resources and deep pockets. He could imagine them picking up where Reynolds left off with a vengeance.

The man who hired him had listened to the argument and disagreed. He pointed out that Reynolds was both a new and a minor figure in the American presence in France. He was part of a modest organization that had limited functions. The French were not fond of foreign agents operating in their country. Although Reynolds wasn't an FBI agent, he worked for one. He assured the hit man that the Americans would create a lot of smoke, but that it would dissipate quickly.

He still didn't agree, but he did understand the concern. If Reynolds had gotten too close, he could have unraveled a highly illegal, highly lucrative, and highly embarrassing enterprise, especially for some very prominent people around the world. Whether or not Reynolds' death would relieve the pressure remained to be seen.

He nodded to the concierge as he left his building, and then he walked, with his dog leading the way on his leash, the two blocks to the shopping district where his tailor was located. As he rounded a corner and walked up the street, he nearly collided with a man backing out of a haberdashery while still talking to the owner. He swerved a bit out of his line of travel, and then, a few steps beyond the man, he staggered. He did not dare to turn to look back at the man, but he had seen and heard enough to know that man was Grant Reynolds.

Showing a great deal of self-control, he continued walking down the street until he felt safe enough to pause to look into a window as if he were window shopping. Finally, he glanced back up the sidewalk.

He had hoped in those few moments that he had been wrong, that the man was simply an American—Americans often looked alike—but his hopes plummeted when he turned back. It was Reynolds. Something had gone terribly wrong. He could only imagine what his client would say when he found the wrong man had been killed.

He was powerless to do anything. He didn't have a gun with him, and he wouldn't be foolish enough to try to kill someone in his own neighborhood. More out of whimsy than desperation, he imagined pushing Reynolds in front of a passing truck, but he knew he was fantasizing. Not only was Reynolds much larger than he, he also had a bodyguard with him. Although he stood off to one side and was dressed in civilian clothes, the Assassin knew a cop when he saw one. The man was a policeman, and he was probably one of the better ones. He stood ready, and he scanned the side-walk and street, twice letting his eyes rest on the older fellow curiously standing in front of a window a few doors down.

He forced himself to move on. He'd have to do without the suit. He might have to do without a lot more. When it became known that he had failed, his reputation would be permanently damaged. He had to do something to salvage what he could. He would have another go at Reynolds. First he would have to find out where he lived. Obviously the man had moved. Finding that out, though, might be difficult. He would have to follow the American to his new address, but with a bodyguard present, that would not be easy. He would have to find another way.

As Grant backed out of the store, he didn't notice the man with the dog who swerved to miss him. He was trying to make sense of what he had learned. He had brought a copy of the only picture he had of The Assassin, the one with his head tipped down that provided the best view of his hat. The store owner, Alain Dubois, had laughed when he saw the picture.

"I've never sold one of those *les chapeaux*. They've been out of style for twenty years."

"Our records show that hats like that were sold from this store," Grant said.

"I'm sure my father sold such things back then, but not in a lot of years. Baseball caps," he said, with disgust. "That's the style of the day. Gentlemen still buy *les chapeaux*, but I'm not sure they ever wear them."

"Do you have your father's records?"

"Long gone. We only keep records the government requires, and at that our records last longer than the governments in France do."

"Would your father remember?" Grant asked.

"I'm sure he would if he were alive."

"Can you think of anyone who could help me?"

"I'm sorry. Let me see that picture again." He looked at it for nearly a minute, and then he handed it back to Grant. "I don't know what it is, but something in the picture is familiar." He was still looking at the picture, so he did not see the man with the dog step aside to avoid Grant.

"Take your time," Grant said.

He shook his head. "I don't know what it is. I'm old enough now that things just pop in and out of my head. Keeping them there is work."

Grant still didn't have his own business cards, but he'd been given a dozen cards with the numbers of the Legat Office on them. He wrote his name on the back of one of the cards and handed it to the man. "If you think of anything, call our office and give them my name. The secretary will put you in touch with me."

He took the card. "Certainly," he said. As an afterthought, he asked, "Can I keep the picture?"

Grant had more copies. "Of course," he said.

As they walked away, Grant asked his bodyguard, "Do we need to get you home? I wouldn't want your boss to think you've gone missing."

"I have a cell phone, Monsieur," he said.

"And an Uzi?"

The man smiled slightly. "I am armed, Monsieur."

Grant glanced at his companion. He was as tall as Grant, but he was a big-boned man with broad shoulders, and he looked like he far outweighed the American. "I hope you're not muscle-bound," Grant mumbled to himself.

He arrived back at the office late in the afternoon, and he found that Dale had kept his word. He was back at his desk with his ear pressed to a phone. When Grant entered, he held up a finger as if to signal him to stay. A few minutes later he hung up the phone and folded his hands on his desktop. He said, "You've been a busy boy since I've been away."

"You know how it is," Grant said, "the mice will play while the rats ..."

Dale cut him off. "We have a serious problem here. Your life appears to be in danger. I've contacted the State Department about having you flown home."

Grant sat on the corner of his desk. He nailed Dale with his eyes until the other man began to squirm, and then he said, "Let's not be stupid," he said, using the word "stupid" intentionally. "First of all, the Assassin has killed people in a lot of countries, including the States. If he's determined to kill me, he'll just go there to do it. Second, he wouldn't be trying to kill me if I wasn't close to something. Third, sending me away might end any chance you have of solving the Tiffany Sutherby murder. Finally, Dale, you're full of shit. I make you nervous. You want me gone."

"You're a loose cannon," Dale sputtered.

"And you're a gone cannon," Grant snapped back. "You're out of the office every chance you get. The fact that I make things happen when you're gone only points out that the work you need to do is here."

"You can't talk to me this way," he said.

"Go back to London, Dale. Enjoy your stay there. There's not a thing here you can do to make things better."

The mention of London was all that Dale needed. The anger faded from his face. "I was in the middle of something important."

"I've got a bodyguard," Grant said, gesturing toward the

hall where the man waited outside the door. "The Assassin will know that he no longer has surprise on his side. He won't try something stupid. I'll be okay."

"In that case," Dale said, "I'll take you up on that. I think I'm being a big help to the London office."

Yup, the London office certainly needs you to go to the British Museum and all the other tourist sites for them. "If we need you, we'll give you a call."

Fifteen minutes later, Dale was packed up and out the door again. Grant decided it was time to go home. He went around and made sure the office was secure, not sure if Jill would be back or not, and then he pulled the gun and shells out of his desk. He stuffed his pockets with bullets, and he slipped the gun back into the back of his pants.

After locking the office door, he started down the stairs, saying to his bodyguard, "Let's go home."

TWENTY-FOUR

He had only been in the apartment for a few minutes when the phone rang. Not the cell phone, but the one that came with the apartment. He thought it might be Gilles Gide. He was wrong. It was Walter Sutherlin.

After the man had introduced himself, Grant asked, "How did you get this number?"

"Through the embassy, of course," Sutherlin said.

He held his anger in check, but he wasn't happy with the embassy. A man had set out to kill him, a man who might well be connected to Sutherlin, and the embassy was still giving out Grant's phone number. Phone numbers could easily be traced to addresses. He was glad he brought the gun home with him.

His bodyguard talked on his cell phone in the kitchen, making arrangements for his replacement, while Grant moved into the living room, thinking another person was about to get his address. To Sutherlin he said, "I'm impressed with your connections."

"I have good friends in government," he said, leaving it at that.

Grant moved to the bedroom and pulled the gun out from the back of his pants. He slipped it under his pillow, and then he transferred the shells in his pocket to the drawer in the bedstand. While doing this he said to Sutherlin, "I appreciate your call. I do have some questions for you."

"I will answer a few questions," he said, "but my lawyers caution me that it's premature to be too cooperative."

What in the hell did that mean? Unless he was guilty of something, he needed neither a lawyer nor a reason not to answer questions. "I understand," he said, without understanding a thing.

"First," Sutherlin said, "I'm a little embarrassed to say this, but I'm afraid that Linda may have given you some misinformation."

"Misinformation from a lawyer?" Grant asked with a straight face.

"Please don't blame her. She is missing some information."

"What is it I'm not going to blame her for?"

"I'm afraid I tried to impress her with my collection of paintings. In doing so I may have misled her."

First, Linda wasn't going to be impressed with his paintings, and with her knowledge of paintings, she could easily mislead herself. "And how is that?"

"I believe she told you I had a Degas, a Chagall, and a Rembrandt?"

"I think those were the artists she mentioned," Grant said, "but in her defense I don't think she paid close attention to your tour of the museum."

"No, no, no, she did get the names right. What she doesn't know, though, is that the paintings are reproductions."

This was an interesting twist. "Reproductions?"

"Yes. I had them commissioned."

"Through Euro-Arts?"

A pause. "Yes. They can discreetly provide startling reproductions."

"With your money, sir, why would you settle for a reproduction?" He hoped billionaires were not sensitive about their money.

"Even with my money, some things are out of reach. Paying a commission to have these reproductions painted was the next best thing. I'm afraid my friends and myself try to impress each other, even if it means cheating a little."

Something didn't sound right to Grant, but he didn't know what it was yet. He changed the subject. "I feel I must ask you if you believe that a connection exists between the death of your granddaughter and yourself."

That pause again. "I would be devastated if such a connection existed," he said.

Grant noted that Walter had not answered his question. "The man who killed your granddaughter also killed an employee of Euro-Arts. The same man made an attempt on my life. I can appreciate odds as much as anyone, but I believe we've gone beyond coincidence. Sir, these deaths have something to do with you."

"I'm afraid I can't comment on that," Walter said. He then seemed to wait expectantly for Grant to ask the right question.

What was the right question? "Considering it's my life that now appears to be in danger, I'm afraid . . ." he let the words sink in, "that you have to comment on that."

"I promise you I had nothing to do with the attempt on your life."

"We only have a few avenues to explore," Grant said. "One is you; the other is Euro-Arts."

No comment. No denial either. "I'm sure you will look where you must," Walter Sutherlin said.

Grant pressed. "If you are not the source of the problem, then that leaves Euro-Arts."

"I didn't say that," Walter said, but he said it in a way that suggested no denial at all.

"Would you suggest we look into Euro-Arts more than we have?"

The pause lasted nearly a minute. He could almost hear Walter thinking on the other end of the line. Finally he said, "I do not want to lose any more of my grandchildren." And then he hung up.

Grant was sure now that he had asked the right questions. Walter had come just short of shouting "Go for Euro-Arts!" He paced in the bedroom. What could it be? Some piece was missing. He thought he had it when Linda listed the painters. None of them had shown up on any of the transactions that Walter had done with Euro-Arts. Now he understood why. If you were buying reproductions and passing them off as originals, then you wouldn't want a public record of it.

It had to be something, though. And it had to be Euro-Arts. And to get people killed, it had to be something big. Grant headed for the kitchen. What in the hell could it be?

In the kitchen, he asked the bodyguard, "You wouldn't happen to be a gourmet cook, would you?"

TWENTY-FIVE

The idea had actually come from seeing an American film. A rather frail young man found himself in a confrontation in a bar with a bully much bigger than himself. More as an act of survival than anything, the frail young man kicked the other man in the testicles when he was least expecting it. As the man sank to his knees, his hand buried in his crotch, the young man used a barstool to knock him senseless.

Leave it to the Americans when it came to violence. The surprise part inspired him, though. He had killed several people that way, in public places, out of the blue. The fact that everyone around was so unprepared for it worked in his favor. Everyone seemed to freeze in shock, and in that brief moment he was able to make his kill and walk away unhindered.

No one, but no one, could imagine the thrill such a killing gave him.

He was about to do it again. He took up a position around the corner from the apartment door. When he heard them arrive, he would simply wait for the sound of the key in the lock, and then he would walk around the corner and shoot them both.

The plan nearly worked perfectly. He heard them speaking softly in French as they entered the building, their voices increasing in volume as the two neared the apartment.

The sound of the footsteps stopped. He could hear keys on a key ring. A key slid into a lock. He spun around the corner, the gun in his hand at the end of a stretched-out arm, and quickly closed the distance between them.

Only then did he realize the distance was too great. The bodyguard was beginning to turn toward him long before he got to her, and the American woman was turning to him too while her hand plunged into her purse.

He was forced to fire from too great a distance, but he was lucky because the first woman dropped to her knees and fell to the floor. The American was thrown off balance as the bodyguard fell at her feet, so when she pulled out the gun and fired, the bullet plowed into the wall a good two feet away from him. The explosion of the shot reverberated in the halls and in his head.

He was not a large man, not much bigger than the woman. Nor was he a man built for physical violence, being slightly overweight. He considered the gun the one item put on earth that could give him an advantage. Her gun took away the advantage.

He was too committed to his plan to change it now. If he tried to turn and run, she could easily shoot him in the back several times before he made it back to the corner. He kept the gun in front of him and continued to fire as he rushed toward her.

She too was firing quickly at him. Neither had the time to aim. He threw himself at her. He had to turn her gun away from him long enough for him to take aim. She fell back, tripping over the bodyguard on the floor, and he fell to his knees, his gun hand caught up in the tangle of arms and legs. This might have been the end for him, but the American woman had lost her gun when she fell. She twisted over on her side and stretched out for the gun that had landed above her head on the floor.

He jerked his hand with the gun in it free, and then he brought it around to aim it at the back of the woman's head. Just as he was about to squeeze off a shot, he heard a metallic click, and his eyes darted to the right just as he pulled the trigger. The bodyguard was still alive and she had her gun.

To his horror, he realized that his shot had missed. The American had reached her gun, and she was beginning to twist back. He was defeated. He pushed himself to his feet and ran back down the hall the way he came, a hail of bullets slamming into the ceiling and walls around him. He made the turn and kept running, amazed that he had not been hit.

Both women fired blindly at him. The bodyguard's vision was blurred by the slug that had mushroomed upon hitting the lower part of her skull. She had turned just enough so that the Assassin's bullet had missed the soft tissue just below the base of the skull, the spot he was aiming for, and had hit solid bone a few inches to the left. The .22 hollow-point shell had flattened against the bone without penetrating the skull. The shock waves, though, had momentarily caused her to black out. When she came to seconds later, she had trouble focusing her eyes as her brain struggled with the jolt it had taken.

Jill was equally lucky and unlucky. The bullet aimed for the back of her head had been redirected when the Assassin glanced away at the last second. The gun could have just as easily jerked to the right, the direction the Assassin looked, but instead he had kept the gun steady, and his hand had dropped an inch as he leaned slightly in the direction he looked. As a result, the bullet had plowed into Jill's back, sliding between two ribs and fragmenting as it went. One fragment had pierced a lung, collapsing it.

She had been writhing in pain and struggling for breath

as she emptied her gun, firing at the retreating figure of the Assassin.

An hour could be a long time—a lifetime—the Assassin thought, as he sipped cognac in his atrium, his dog curled at his feet. And then, suddenly, minutes. Time was an odd thing that never had the order to it in the mind that it had in the external world.

The whole madcap scene replayed itself over and over in his head. He struggled with the sudden notion that he had indeed lost it. Whatever brilliant edge he had before was gone, and if he still might have some doubt about that, he knew the people who hired him wouldn't. This last episode would put him permanently out of work.

He wanted to slap his forehead and moan about what-*had*-he-been-thinking, but he was not one for self-recrimination. A tactic that worked so well for him before had failed this time. If the distance from the corner had been fifteen feet instead of twenty, both women would be dead now. If he had simply walked around the corner with a pleasant smile on his face, tipping his hat to the women as he approached, he might have disarmed them long enough to get closer and then the tactic would have succeeded. He could have even let himself into the apartment and waited for them to enter, catching them completely unprepared.

So many other things he could have done … . He sat, stunned, nursing his cognac. This was a first for him. Never had so many things gone so wrong.

He pulled his cell phone from his pocket and dialed the number. He would do his best to put a positive spin on it. He would tell his client that he had failed to kill Reynolds, but he had done the next best thing. His attack on Reynolds' partner would send a message. Reynolds would back off. They agreed that these messages worked. Surely Reynolds would get the message.

The Assassin has miscalculated one more time. Grant Reynolds wasn't intimidated by the message; he was furious. He was mad in a cold, hollow, empty way. He was so full of fury that only one thing would appease it: He would find the Assassin and kill him.

Grant leaned against the hallway wall and watched the police in action, Gerard directing the scene. Jill's bodyguard was still at the scene, on a stretcher, but able to answer questions put to her by Gerard and his men. In these moments he worked hard to suppress the emotions that could well lead to him doing something foolish. Emotions had to be buried if intellect was to be allowed to do its job. He knew though, from years of experience, that burying emotions came with a price.

A few moments later, Jill's stretcher was carried to an ambulance, with Grant walking beside it, holding her hand. Jill was in a great deal of distress, in part because of bullet in her back, and in part because of the gun. The gun caused Gerard considerable distress, too. Everyone seemed more concerned about the gun than the attack by the Assassin.

After the ambulance had left and he had returned to the hallway, Grant found out just how important the gun was. Gerard ordered Grant's bodyguard to pat him down to see if he was carrying a gun as well. Fortunately, after the call came in, Grant had left too fast to get to the scene of the shooting to take the time to retrieve the gun under his pillow.

After Gerard had talked to his policewoman and then released her to go to the hospital, after he had overseen the bagging of Jill's gun, and after he had given instructions to everyone there, he finally came to Grant. He was not a happy man.

"Your officer?" Grant asked.

"Like being hit on the head with a baseball bat. A concussion maybe, but no worse than that. And Jill?"

"Lung collapsed. Fingers and toes work. A lot of pain." Years as a homicide detective probably qualified him to do triage. He'd seen enough shot people in his day. "I'm guessing surgery and an extended recovery period because of the lung, but barring complications I think she'll be okay."

Gerard nodded, the sadness still there, in the eyes. "The gun is a complication. I hope you understand that."

"You can't bury it under the carpet? You know, extenuating circumstances?"

"Your request for gun permits, your warning about carrying a gun, this gun itself, all are now documented. Given the climate between the French and the Americans, I can promise you it will not go unnoticed."

"What will happen?"

He shook his head and shrugged. "I will do everything I can to see that the worst that happens to her is that she is deported."

"You can't go for a warning or a reprimand?"

"I will be lucky to keep her out of jail."

"And you don't see anything wrong in that? She was defending her life against a man who was trying to kill her. For all you know, that gun may be the only reason the two of them are alive."

"I'm sorry," Gerard said. "It's not that simple."

Grant gave up the argument. He wasn't on his turf. This was an issue that would be played out by diplomats. He knew, though, that Jill would have to pay a price, and he also knew he was the one who had encouraged her to carry the gun. "Did you get a description?" Grant asked.

"You may have heard this before. Raincoat, floppy hat with rim pulled low over the eyes. Gun with a silencer. We will have to wait until Jill is in less pain to see if she can add to that."

"The Assassin."

"You're a former policeman. We'll need more to prove that, as obvious as it seems to us."

Now that he had brought his emotions back into check, Grant had to agree that Gerard was right. It could have been someone else. In his mind, though, he had no doubt. If the Assassin couldn't kill Grant, he would send him a message by way of Jill. He knew how the Assassin worked.

"I'm going to the hospital," Grant said.

"Wait a few minutes. I have a relief coming for your bodyguard. He will drive you."

Grant nodded. Then he thought of how much good Jill's bodyguard had been. He immediately felt bad about the thought. For all he knew, she might be the reason Jill was still alive. "Will you be coming, too?" he asked.

"Later. I don't think she will be in a condition to talk to either of us until tomorrow."

Gerard was right, of course. Still, Grant felt he needed to be there for her. He gave a quick wave of his hand and started to walk outside to wait for his ride. Behind him, he heard Gerard say, "And Grant, do not make it worse. No more guns."

TWENTY-SIX

The only coherent thought that emerged from her fog-filled brain was that she now understood what Grant had meant by the blink of an eye. If she had not glanced to the left at just the right moment, if she had not been putting her keys back in her purse, if the gun had not come so quickly to her hand ... all of it was so fast.

She was trying to remember what the man had looked like. She wanted to tell Grant. The face would not materialize through the fog, just the eyes. She wouldn't forget the eyes. How calm they were; how devoid of emotion. He was trying to kill her, and his eyes seemed to say, "Nothing personal—just business."

Her first shot was the only one she remembered. If she had waited longer, she would have had the gun around and would have hit him. But it all happened too fast. She struggled to remember it, but nothing came from the fog but a blurry image of bodies falling, thundering gun shots in the closed space, and wrestling on the floor—for the gun, for a shot, for life.

From the fog came voices, too. Nurses and doctors. Grant reassuring her that she would be okay, that her bodyguard had been even more fortunate with only a small wound to heal and a large headache to get rid of.

She began to drift back to sleep. She fought it, trying to remember if there had been any other voices. Had the man said anything? Had she screamed? Had the body-guard screamed? Nothing. It was a life and death drama, and not a word had been spoken. She thought she might have grunted when the bullet hit her in the back, but that was the only sound she could remember coming from any of them. The booming of the guns, though, she knew she would never forget.

Grant had stayed at the hospital until she had come out of surgery. An hour later, when she was stable in recovery, they let him have two minutes with her. He held her hand and reassured her that she was okay, that the police officer was okay. And, before he was told he must go, he assured her that he would get The Assassin. The man had killed his last victim, he promised.

After he left the hospital, he went home to shower and shave, and then he grabbed a few hours' sleep. He was up early and off to the office before the light of dawn, a fact that didn't make his bodyguards very happy. Yes, now he had two of them.

As they neared the office, one of the bodyguards went ahead and checked the doorways and alleyways, signal-ing them to follow when things were clear. At the office building, one went up first, checking the staircase and the hallways before telling the other to come up on a walkie-talkie. Grant was a little impatient with all this, sure that the Assassin wouldn't make the same mistake twice, but he also understood the caution. It had been a cop who had been shot as well as Jill.

Grant spent the first hours in the office writing reports. They would have to be done anyway, but he used writing them as a means to review everything that had happened. He was still trying to make sense of it all. Although it was easy to get caught up in the search for the Assassin, he also knew that he was investigating two cases. One would hopefully lead to the Assassin; the second case involved Tiffany Sutherby's death. The Assassin had killed her, but Grant still didn't know why she had been killed or who had ordered her death. He was sure who did it, but he couldn't prove that without knowing the why.

Sutherlin and Euro-Arts. That was the connection. But what was the connection? He bought paintings from them, and commissioned copies of masterpieces. Where in that was a reason for someone to get murdered?

He had a thought. Not even a complete thought. More like a vague idea. He couldn't even begin to give it shape without more information. He picked up his phone and called Linda Ebenhart's number.

She answered on the first ring. "God, I was hoping it would be you," she said. "I heard."

"How did you find out?" He tried to keep the suspicion out of his voice, but he was too tired to be diplomatic.

"You don't suspect me in this, too, do you?" she asked, the hurt obvious in her voice.

"I'm sorry," he said. "It's been a long night and I'm grasping at straws right now. I've got to stop this man."

"I saw it on the front page of a paper when I went jogging. It had a picture of Jill. I bought a copy, but my French is so bad … I had the desk clerk read the story to me. I'm so sorry. How is she?"

"It will take awhile, but she'll be okay. I don't think she'll like the surgery scar on her back, though."

"There is such a thing as plastic surgery," Linda said.

"I'm sure she'll think about that."

"Are you okay?"

"It wasn't me he shot."

"You know what I mean." He did, and he didn't want to think about it. He had stopped off at the church to pray for Jill after he left the hospital. He had lit candles for the dead.

He still lit a candle for the boy he'd killed every chance he got. No, he wasn't okay. He might never be okay.

"I won't be okay until I get the Assassin. I won't be okay until I know who killed Tiffany, and why. I need to talk to Walter again," he said.

"Is that why you called?"

"Yes," he said. "No," he said, not sure why he added that.

"Is it something we can talk about?"

"In time, maybe. Right now I need to talk to Walter."

"He won't talk to you."

"What is he afraid of? Is he afraid that someone will try to kill him? Is he afraid that he might have done something that will land him in jail? What is it? I was sure the last time I talked to him that he was the key to all of this. Why won't he talk to me?"

"He told you why."

"He doesn't want to lose any more of his grandchildren?"

"Yes."

"Why is he so afraid that will happen?"

"Grant, you have to believe me. I don't know what's going on any more than you do. He only gives me pieces of a puzzle because he's so afraid for his grandchildren. By the way, he's hired bodyguards for each of them."

"Are you sure he's not afraid for himself?"

"I'm positive."

"How can you be so sure?"

"He's dying, Grant. He has cancer. It's inoperable. He has maybe three months. Maybe less." Now he understood why his legacy, his children and his grandchildren, were suddenly so important to him. And Grant understood, too, that someone else had figured that out and was using it to manipulate Walter. But why?

"If he won't talk to me, I need you to get some information for me from him."

"If I can."

"I want to know the artists and the titles of the paintings that he commissioned Euro-Arts to have painted for him, and I want to know the names of the people who own Euro-Arts. I want to know who's at the top."

"He might give you the titles of the paintings, but he's made it clear to me that he won't answer any questions about Euro-Arts."

Another confirmation that Euro-Arts was at the heart of this. "I need the names—de Bienne, the man who was killed who worked for Euro-Arts, was insignificant. The man I talked to, Kyle Hosteller, seems to be a mouthpiece and on the fringes and no one will tell me who's at the top. If Walter won't talk to me, then I need to talk to Euro-Arts, and not Kyle Hosteller."

"He won't tell you. You must have your own resources."

Christ, he thought, he had only been in Paris for a couple of weeks now. He wasn't exactly knee-deep in sources, and the ones he had, Gerard and Smith, didn't know who was at the head of Euro-Arts. "If nothing else, get me the names of the paintings, even if you have to break into his museum to do it."

She laughed. "Do you remember how many times I set off my car alarm? I'm not exactly gifted when it comes to breaking and entering."

No, she wasn't one to be clandestine. "Beg him for me. Tell him I think I'm getting close. Tell him I've got a score to settle and I need his help."

"Appeal to his competitive spirit?"

"If he's a billionaire, he's got one."

"I'll do what I can. Have lunch with me?"

"The shit hasn't hit the fan yet, here, but it's early. It will soon. And then I'll need to go to the hospital."

"To see Jill?"

"Yes."

"Is there something there I should know about?"

Women always asked the right question, which was the wrong one to ask. "I've only been here two weeks," he said.

"I fell in love with you after two days."

He did not want to go there. He knew he hadn't dealt with all that very well at the time, and he knew he had tried to bury it unsuccessfully while it was still alive. On his shelf was a dead girlfriend, and the boy he had shot, and maybe Jill soon. He was rapidly developing a life filled with prayers and candles. Like all those other things, he had to admit now that Linda was on the shelf, too, and like the others she refused to be buried in the past.

"Please get the information for me." He hung up the phone.

The door burst open and Dale walked in. His little display of temper caused both bodyguards to draw their weapons and point them at Dale, who froze in his tracks with his hands in the air; he turned quite white. Grant held up a hand. "You might do us all a favor if you shot him," he said, "but he's with me."

"That's not funny," Dale said, cautiously lowering his hands. Once he saw it was okay, he placed his briefcase on his desk and walked into the conference room. When Grant followed him in, he found Dale opening the safe. He smiled to himself. He knew what he was looking for.

Dale found the one gun and pulled it out. He turned to glare at Grant. Grant only smiled at him and said, "Try the drawer on the bottom."

Dale pulled open the drawer and found the other gun. The steam seemed to go out of him. "If you had had that gun on you, it would have been over for you here."

Grant had figured that out last night. When he came back to work early in the morning, it was to make sure he arrived before anyone else showed up. That gave him time to slip the gun back into the safe. As much as he hated the idea, he would have to search for the Assassin unarmed.

Grant was back at his desk for only a few moments when his phone rang. He answered it. The ambassador was on the other end.

"Good morning, sir," he said.

"Grant, this is disturbing news. What's the latest on Ms. St. Claire?"

"The bullet was a small caliber. It fragmented when it hit a rib. One fragment punctured a lung. That seems to be the worst of it. The doctors repaired the damage. She'll need some recovery time," he added.

"Unfortunate, unfortunate. Especially about the gun. The French are very unreasonable about that."

"If she hadn't been armed, sir," Grant said, "I believe she would be dead now."

"Let me assure you that the French don't always listen to reason."

"I'm sure Jill will expect your support, sir. She's very good at her job, and she put her life at risk investigating the death of Tiffany Sutherby. She understood how much both you and the President were concerned about that death."

"Of course, of course. We'll be standing behind her one hundred percent."

"I wouldn't expect anything less of you, sir."

"Will you be seeing her soon?"

"This afternoon."

"Give her my best wishes. Assure her that we will do everything we can with the French. I'm ordering my secretary now to send flowers."

"She'll appreciate that, sure."

"Do you think we should send you back to the States for your own safety?" he asked.

"The attacker is a man we call the Assassin. He's killed people all over the world. I don't know that I'd be any safer back home than I am here. Besides, that would leave just Dale to run the office."

"I see what you mean," he said. "You will be careful?"

"I have two of France's finest in the office with me now."

"Good, good, well, keep me appraised."

Grant set down the receiver and let out a slow breath. One bullet dodged.

"Way to manipulate the ambassador," Dale said. "He's not a stupid man. He'll see what you were doing."

"I only asked him to do his job," Grant said. "Besides, he wanted to send me back to the States and leave you here alone in the office. No telling when the Assassin will want to try to pop you."

Dale paled again. "He must know I have nothing to do with this investigation," he stuttered.

"Why would he? He's gone after everyone else in this office."

Dale sank down in his chair and shut up. Grant had given him something unpleasant to think about. Grant turned his head away so Dale couldn't see the smile on his face.

His phone rang again, and this time he knew he had nothing to smile about. It was the Legal Attaché. Mark Trumbo was a career agent. He had climbed the ladder and proven himself competent every step of the way. When the agency was taking a hit because an agent was caught spying for the Russians, Trumbo shined. He was the one who had done the catching.

His reward was a plum assignment among agents. Only the best got Legal Attaché positions, and only the very best got them in prime spots like Paris. He might be able to manipulate the ambassador, but he wasn't going to fool Trumbo.

"Good morning, sir," he said.

"I've got to give you credit, Reynolds, you know how to stir up dust."

"Just doing my job, sir," Grant said.

"I think you're doing more than your job," Trumbo said. "I think you're still a homicide cop."

"Are we not, at any given moment, an accumulation of everything we were before?" It was probably the wrong thing to say, Grant knew, but if Trumbo was a cop, too, he would know what Grant was saying.

"You can take the cop to the city but you can't take the cop out of the cop?" Trumbo asked.

"I want this guy, sir. I know I'm getting close or shots wouldn't have been fired, and I think I'm beginning to understand what's going on."

"You don't know how precarious of a position you're in. This had better be good."

The idea came even more into focus as he explained it to Trumbo. The agent would either think he was a fool, or his cop instinct would understand what he was saying. So he went over his theory on why he thought the man was French, the identified hat connection, and his ideas about the Assassin's work drying up.

When Grant finished, Trumbo asked, "But how does that explain the death of Sutherlin's granddaughter?"

"I'm still working on that."

"Can you prove any of it?"

"I need the names of Sutherlin's paintings, and then I need to find out who the head of Euro-Arts is and talk to him."

"Do you know the implications of what you're saying?"

"If I'm right, sir, and I can prove it, I suspect some important people around the world will be doing a little cheek clenching."

Silence. That was soon followed by a low chuckle. "I'll

have to remember that," he said. "I might even use it with the President, because he's going to want to know. He'll want to separate himself from anything embarrassing."

"He might have a few people to worry about, but the rest will be someone else's problem."

"I was glad when they hired you, Grant. I want your office to do more and be for more than just holding American hands. You pull this off and I see some major changes ahead. Screw it up and you're on your way out."

"It's been like that all my life," Grant said.

Trumbo chuckled louder this time. "Mine, too. Go have coffee with that buddy Gilles Gide of yours. He'll know who's at the top of Euro-Arts."

"That may be, but last time I talked to him he didn't want to give out names. Clients."

"I guess you will find out just how good of a buddy he is, then, won't you?"

"Yes sir."

"Is Dale still there?"

"Yes."

"Tell him to go back to London. I know that if anyone shoots him here, it'll be an accident, but I'd just as soon have him out of harm's way."

"Yes sir."

After he had hung up, Dale said, "Rubbing elbows with the higher-ups, now?"

"Trumbo said for you to go back to London."

Dale brightened. "Really?"

"Really."

Reaching for his briefcase, he asked, "Are you sure you won't be needing me?"

He was out the door before Grant had a chance to answer. He didn't have much time to enjoy the quiet. His phone rang again and this time it was James Smith.

"Was it the Assassin?" Smith asked first off.

Grant made himself comfortable behind his desk. This looked like one of those days he was destined to spend on the phone. "I don't think there's any doubt, although we don't have a clean description yet. The woman police officer who was shot was just turning to him when she got hit in the head. Fortunately for her, the bullet flattened and didn't penetrate the skull. She never saw anything in focus after that.

"I haven't had a chance to talk to Jill, yet. My guess is she didn't see much either. The woman cop saw a raincoat, hat pulled low over the eyes, and a gun with a silencer on it. I don't think we've much doubt."

"Why Jill?"

"My guess is that when he failed to get to me, he decided to reach me in the same way that he sent a message to Euro-Arts. He decided to kill Jill."

"Does he really think you'll back off?"

"I think what we've seen in the last week is a desperate man. He's scrambling to save his reputation as a hit man, and everything he's doing is making him look bad."

"What does that mean to us?"

"It means he's as vulnerable now as he's ever been. I think we only have one chance to get him. After this I think he goes into retirement; if we haven't caught him by then, we won't catch him once he does."

"Anything new?"

Grant tried out his theory on Smith. This time, it became even clearer to Grant than it had been when he told it to the Legal Attaché.

Once he was finished, Smith didn't have much to say for several moments. Finally he said, "I like it. I like it. I like it because it answers a lot of questions about a lot of things. The only remaining question is, what did Sutherlin do to get his granddaughter killed?"

"I think I know the answer to that, too, but only Sutherlin can confirm it. Right now he's not talking. As long as the Assassin is on the loose, I don't think he will talk either. We need to get the Assassin."

"Any ideas?"

"I'm still working on it."

"Anything I can do?"

"Not until we get a break."

Grant hung up the phone. Almost immediately it rang again, and with it came the break.

Grant wasn't surprised. A homicide detective went out and cast line after line in the places where a clue might be. Over time he reeled in the lines. Most of the time they came in empty. Occasionally they came in with a gem on the end. This line came with a gem, but a small one.

On the other end of the line was Alain Dubois. He said, "I don't know if this will be of any help, but I keep seeing a resemblance every time I look at the picture you left."

Grant wasn't about to get excited. Often people were so eager to help the police they imagined things that might be of use. "How so?" he asked.

"It's not the hat and it's not the coat, but it's something in the bearing of the man."

Now Grant began to take more interest. He knew that the Assassin would not wear the hat and coat he used in the hits unless he was on his way to kill someone. Dubois wouldn't have seen him in this hat and coat. "What about the bearing?"

"Every once in a while I see a man from the neighborhood out walking his dog. When the weather is bad, he wears a coat that looks a bit like this one, and he's fond of hats with wide brims. Of course I would notice the hat. In this picture, the man is walking, his right arm swinging out. It reminds me of this man holding the leash of his dog.

The slight tilt of the head, the slight stoop to the shoulders, the hunching down as if to look smaller: they are all the same."

"What kind of a dog?"

Dubois brightened. "I had one once myself. A Scottish Terrier."

"Do you know the man's name or where he lives?"

"I know neither, but I do know this is primarily a business district. We have hotels and only a few apartments nearby. The apartments are quite expensive. The man must live only a few blocks away."

"How can you be sure of that?"

"I notice clothing more than I notice people. A few times I have noticed when it is raining that this man when I see him is not very wet. I just guessed that he must have come from indoors not far from my store."

"That's a wonderful observation," Grant said. "Can you tell me anything else about the man?"

"No, not really. He is in his forties, maybe a bit older. He seems to be of medium build and to be overweight, but that is hard to tell for sure because of the coat. I cannot tell you much about his face because of the hat. He wasn't a man to look you straight on."

"Did you ever see him without the dog?"

Grant could tell that Dubois was giving this careful thought. So far he had been the kind of witness that cops dream about. When he spoke it was with confidence. "I once saw him come out of the tailor shop down the street. I noticed specifically because he didn't have the dog."

"Thank you very much," Grant said. "If you can remember anything else, please let me know."

"I hope I've been a help."

"I think you have. I really think you have."

Grant motioned to his guards that he was about to

leave. First he would swing by the hospital to see how Jill was doing, and then he would look for the tailor shop. "I think we'll need a car," Grant said, and then smiled when he saw one of the police officers call from his cell phone. If only getting a car from the embassy motor pool were so easy, he thought.

He had in the past a thousand promising leads dry up and blow away. He wasn't getting his hopes up. Even if they could identify the man, it was quite possible that he wasn't the Assassin. Worse, even if the man was the Assassin, proving it might be nearly impossible. He could take the only action he knew, and that was to follow the lead to see where it went; to keep following it until it led him somewhere or it proved to be useless.

He was only able to spend a few minutes with Jill. She was still groggy and very tired. She seemed glad to see him, but at the same time there was something remote about her. She had been someplace he had not been.

"I'm getting closer," he said. "I just need a few more pieces. Did you get a look at him?"

Jill slowly ran her tongue along her very dry lips. At that moment, without her makeup and with her hair a tangle on the pillow, Grant could see the middle-aged woman that would emerge from her youth. She would fight it, he knew, but she wouldn't like what she would become.

Finally, she said, "I saw his eyes."

"Do you know what color they were?"

"Ice," she said.

"That's not quite a color," he said.

"His eyes were like ice. If a man is going to try to kill you, you'd expect anger, or hate, or fear, or even lust in his eyes. This man's eyes were ice."

"Can you tell me something about his size?"

"The gun and the eyes: those were the only things I saw."

From the haunted look on her face, Grant was sure that those were the only images she would be seeing for a long time to come. Grant knew. Right after he had shot the boy, even in the dark of the alley he could see the kid's eyes go wide with the recognition of his own death. He still saw that face in his dreams.

"Listen," he said. "You need rest. I'll come back tomorrow."

She nodded her head, a slight movement. She was someplace else again, a place located somewhere between her medication and her nightmares. He bent down and kissed her on the forehead, but she didn't seem to notice.

Damn, he thought, as we walked with his bodyguards back to the car. People survived all sorts of traumas, but they really *didn't* survive them. The moment passed only to return over and over again to haunt them. He knew. And he didn't know how to shake it off. He could see that Jill was in for the same kind of journey he had taken.

The tailor shop was only a few doors down from the hat shop. Grant found it easily, but he discovered questioning the owner wasn't going to be as easy as Dubois had been. This fellow spoke very poor English. He was forced to use one of his bodyguards to translate, which was only marginally better. Neither of the men spoke fluent English.

Between his rudimentary French and their rudimentary English, he did get his questions answered. Yes, once he understood the description, the owner knew who the man was. Yes, the one with the dog. Yes, a Scottish Terrier. The man had told him the breed. Yes, he was a long-time customer, although he hadn't ordered a new suit in a while. He used to order on a regular basis.

Grant wanted to know if the man knew why the customer had not ordered a new suit in a while. This took the greatest effort on everyone's part, but finally Grant was made to understand that the tailor thought that the man had suffered financial reversals.

Ten minutes later they left the shop with the name of the customer and his address, an apartment building a few blocks away. Grant asked the cops to drive him there, and once they were parked across from the building he sent one of them inside to ask a question of the manager.

Both men looked at him as if he were an idiot when he told them the question he wished answered. Grant stayed in the car. He would let the French cop and the French apartment manager struggle with the question.

Five minutes later the cop returned to the car, a scowl on his face. Inside, he simply said his question had not earned much respect for the police, but he had gotten the answer.

Six stories up, Maurice Beauchamp stood in his window and watched the car parked across the street below. He knew it was a police car. He knew the man who got out of it was a police officer. Although he could not make out the others in the car, he was sure that one of them would be Grant Reynolds. He had heard Reynolds' name repeated several times during his last phone conversation. Reynolds knew, his client said, and now he was out to prove what he knew. Beauchamp's bungling had only made it worse and if something wasn't done immediately ... He didn't finish the thought. Apparently his client could not even stand to verbalize the possible consequences.

Beauchamp had said nothing. He knew it was too late. He had realized after the fact that killing the woman wouldn't have changed anything. He would have had to kill Reynolds, and he would have had to do that days ago to stop what he was sure was going to happen. As he watched the car pull away, he knew it was time to leave.

Back at his office, Grant got on the phone and called Gerard. He explained briefly what he had been up to, and then asked Gerard to find out something for him.

Gerard's response was comic. "You want me, a senior police detective, to investigate a dog?"

Grant smiled. "I sent one of your men in to ask the apartment manager if he knew what Monsieur Beauchamp did with his dog when he traveled. We learned from the tailor that Monsieur Beauchamp is quite close to his dog, and he has had this pet for about twelve years."

"Yes, and Hitler liked little children, but what has this got to do with identifying Beauchamp as the Assassin?"

"We need to find out from the kennel the dates he left the dog. If I'm right and this is the Assassin, then those dates will correspond roughly to the dates of a hit by the Assassin somewhere in the world."

He could hear the sharp intake of breath at the other end of the line. "That's quite brilliant," Gerard said.

"And if the correlation exists, you must promise me that you'll take me with you when you go to interview the man."

"If the correlation exists, I will carry you there on my shoulders," Gerard said.

TWENTY-SEVEN

Despite a day filled with so many things happening at once, Grant did have time for dinner with Linda. He called and she accepted, even though he apologized to her because they would have to eat in her hotel restaurant again. His bodyguards were not keen about trying to protect him while he was out on the town.

Again she met him in the lobby. She wore an evening gown that hugged her body, something in light green that looked like it was made out of silk. She wore her hair the same way as before with that just-woke-up look, but a thin gold necklace seemed to make it all work. God, she was lovely. He glanced at his two bodyguards. They looked like they wanted to search her and not for a weapon.

She took in the two bodyguards and asked, "Will they be joining us?"

"Separate tables," he said. "I promised them a dinner on me."

"Considering the price of meals here, you're being very generous," she said, taking his arm.

"Considering that I am still alive," he responded, "they're worth it."

Arranging the tables wasn't as easy as it seemed. The bodyguards wanted the two of them against a wall and out of sight of the windows. They then wanted to be between Grant and Linda and the entrance. It took all the French that Linda and Grant knew to understand and accept what the guards ordered the waiters to do to arrange it all.

Once they were settled in and had ordered, Linda asked, "How is Jill?"

That was a good question, one for which Grant did not have an answer. She was still in shock from being shot. With that came a certain amount of pain that even the drugs could not completely eliminate. On top of that was the realization that she was in trouble because of the gun. She had been distant with Grant in the hospital, and he didn't think that would change even in time. Grant was far down the list of things which she would need to deal with in the near future.

He had called her mother from the office and told her about the shooting. She was probably on a plane now, heading to Paris. He was able to reassure her mother that Jill would recover completely from her wound, but he knew he'd be deceiving himself if he thought it was true. She would not recover psychologically for a long time to come.

"She's gone through a lot, and she has a lot more to go through," he said. "To be honest, I'm not sure how she is. She's not talking about it right now."

"Will she stay in Paris?"

"I don't think the choice will be hers. The French officials are upset because she was carrying a gun. Our people are defending her, but I wouldn't be surprised if they didn't reassign her for her own good. Paris won't be quite the same for her after this."

Linda was watching the expressions unfold on his face with interest. "If she leaves, will you miss her?"

"Yes," he said. "At the very least, she was good at her job. I appreciate the professionalism. Besides that, she is a nice person. I appreciate that, too."

"And an attractive woman, too," Linda added.

"Frosting, but not the cake," he said.

She continued to watch him, her curiosity obvious. "Will they send you back, too?"

He finally stopped focusing on his hands as he answered these questions and looked at Linda. He knew her well enough that he was sure she wasn't prying for prying's sake. She wanted to know how it was going to be. If he was reassigned to the right spot, he imagined her thinking, maybe they could continue to see each other. If he was going to follow Jill, then she'd live without him. She had before. He reconsidered. Maybe that was too harsh. Maybe Linda had some other agenda.

"I'm pretty sure I'll be staying here."

He watched her face. She didn't even blink. "Paris is a lovely place to be."

Their food arrived and was served. The conversation did not resume until both had eaten part of their meals. He was the one to start it again. "What about you? What happens once Sutherlin dies?"

"Do you mean am I out a job?" The question was rhetorical. "That's hard to say. Walter wants his grandson to take over the business, but he's obviously not ready yet. His son-in-law could probably take the reins and keep things status quo. More than likely a committee will be put together to run things. Scott Sutherby might keep me on; the committee would not."

"If you're out of a job, then what?"

"Oh, I'll most likely go into practice, or maybe, on a whim, start my own. Why don't you join me and actually put that law degree to use?"

He imagined that the two of them would have the perfect relationship if Linda were his boss, at least in her mind. He could see them forever defending socialites for pot busts.

"I just started this job. I'm not tired of it, yet," he said. "I'm not ready to be a lawyer."

No, he hadn't given up the idea of being a lawyer. He didn't work that hard for something and then give it up. He had to step back from it, that was all. The shooting of the boy had put too many lawyers in his life, and not all of them were altruistic.

The boy. How different his life would have been if he had held his fire.

"And you cannot be seduced by money?"

That was another reason why the two of them were not a good mix. Money was always near the top of Linda's priority list. The funny thing about that was, she already had more than he would ever make in a lifetime, and she was still trying to figure out how to get more. In comparison, he had very little, yet he still hadn't figured out how to spend that.

"You know about me and money," he said.

"You truly have a genetic flaw there." She didn't smile when she said this.

They finished their meal in relative quiet, both aware that it was unlikely that the two of them would have many more dinners together.

At the end of the meal, after dessert, she reached into her handbag and pulled out a folded slip of paper. She shoved it across the table to him.

"The list of paintings?"

"Walter is impressed with you."

"Tell Walter that I think we will arrest the killer of his granddaughter soon. Maybe even tomorrow."

"I think he will be relieved. He did say to tell you that he thought you could figure it out from here."

Grant glanced at the list. He didn't recognize the artists or the names of all their paintings, but he recognized enough. He was sure he had already figured it out. "He has more than I thought he would."

"He was a good customer," she said.

Grant paid for the meals with a credit card, and he was forced to admire the audacity of his bodyguards. They truly ate French. The truffles alone would pinch his salary for a month.

They stopped at the elevator. Linda said, "I would invite you up, but I can imagine your two friends standing in the hall with their ears pressed to the door."

"No," he said, laughing, "they would expect to be in the same room with us."

"Not my idea of romance," she said.

No, not his either. Nor was the idea of romance with Linda in the picture. He changed the subject. "Thank you for your help," he said.

She stepped into his arms and kissed him on the lips. She took her time, enjoying the moment despite the guards' interest. "You're welcome," she said when she stepped away. "Don't wrap this up too quickly or I'll have to go home."

He didn't want to say anything to encourage her to stay. On the other hand, a few days of vacation with Linda in Paris might have been a dream of his at one time. "I have a feeling Walter is going to need you," he said.

"Is this going to come back at him in some way?" she asked.

"He knows it will," he said.

"Then this may be goodbye."

"Probably," he said.

She looked like she wanted to kiss him again, but this time she turned and pushed the button to the elevator. She did not turn back.

Grant could tell as the three of them walked out the door that the combination of an expensive meal and the sight of him being kissed by a beautiful woman impressed the two men. As they got to the car, he said, "I need to stop at the office for a few minutes, and then I'll be going home."

As proof of his new status, one of the men opened the door of the car for him.

He only spent a short time at the office. He needed to log onto the Internet. Within a short time he had the information he needed. He silently thanked the FBI and Interpol for their efficiency.

When he let himself into the courtyard with the two guards in tow, he noticed that the lights in the main house were still on. That was good. He wanted to talk to Gilles Gide this evening. He needed a few minutes, though, to frame his thoughts. He understood attorney/client privilege. He didn't think he would be asking any questions that would violate the privilege. What concerned him was that Gilles might say something to his client that could make all of this more difficult.

In his apartment, Grant settled the two bodyguards in the living room while he used the phone in the bedroom to call Gilles. The lawyer answered after two rings.

"This is Grant. I'd like to talk to you this evening if you have a few minutes."

"I could use a break," Gilles said. "I'm preparing for a trial in a case that does not look good for my client."

"If I come there," Grant said, "I'll have to drag my bodyguards with me."

"Let's meet in the courtyard. I could use the air."

A few minutes later the two of them sat on the steps leading up to the front door of Gilles's house. The bodyguards, reluctantly, stood by the gate leading to the street, far enough away so they could not overhear the conversation between Gilles and Grant.

Gilles brought with him a bottle of cognac and two glasses. The men sat in the dark and sipped their drinks. Neither seemed in a hurry to say anything.

Finally, Gilles asked, "That attractive woman?"

He meant Jill. "She will be okay in time."

"A problem with a gun?"

Grant smiled. Gilles would know all of the details. He was a very good lawyer with a lot of reach.

"Inspector Gerard is talking about criminal prosecution. The embassy is saying that she will be deported at least."

"I'll see what I can do," Gide said.

Grant tried to see the features of the man's face, but he had left the porch light off, and the courtyard was only dimly lit. "You have that kind of influence?"

"I have so much influence that I scare a lot of people in important positions." He said it in such a matter-of-fact way that Grant didn't doubt the truth of it for a moment.

"She was carrying a gun," Grant said.

"The paperwork was in the system. Her life, obviously, was in danger. The security put in place obviously wasn't enough. French courts are not unreasonable, and French officials do not like to go to court if they know they will lose. I think I might be able to arrange something."

"I would appreciate anything you might be able to do, but please don't make Gerard the goat."

"The goat?" Gide asked, amused by the idea.

"The sacrifice," Grant said.

"I won't, but don't feel sorry for Gerard. He has his own influence. Why would you care?"

Grant was honest. "I like him, and he's useful."

"Like me," Gide said.

"Both are true, but I have a feeling that I will be played like a harp in your hands over time."

Gide laughed at that. "You will be useful, too. I think

that might be the basis for a good friendship between us in time."

"I don't mean to test that theory so soon," Grant said, "but I do need to know something, and you may be the only one who can tell me."

Gide refilled their glasses carefully in the dark. "I'm listening," he said.

"I need to know who the boss or owner is at Euro-Arts."

"I told you of a possible conflict of interest."

"And I need to know your involvement in Euro-Arts." Grant was surprised at himself. That last part caused him to turn tense. He wasn't sure if he wanted to know the answer to it.

"You mean, am I a client? Or, do I own interest in the company? Or, am I aware of illegal activities that the business might be involved in?"

"All of those."

"What do you think?"

"I think what you told me the first time was true, but now I need to hear it officially from you."

"You must be close to something."

"I can't say."

"Other than representing the company in legal transactions, I have no other involvement with Euro-Arts. As I said before, I am not a customer nor am I a client. And, no, I do not know of any illegal transactions by the company, but let's be realistic. Would Euro-Arts want someone like me to know that the company was doing something illegal? Is that satisfactory?"

"And the name of the head guy?"

"He is a client."

"And you are reluctant to give me his name."

"Reluctant, yes, because from what I gather, I may have

to represent him again in something more serious than arranging a sale."

"I'll be honest with you," Grant said. "I have to worry that anything I say to you might get passed on."

"That's a legitimate concern. You're not my client."

"So I'm not going to get the name?"

Gide breathed deeply of the night air. "You could almost believe, if you used your imagination, that we were in the countryside instead of in the heart of Paris. Illusion is a wonderful thing. In truth little is the way we think it is. We wear many masks for as many different reasons."

Grant wondered if this was Gide's way of changing the subject. He was a complex man, the kind of man that Grant liked the most. Not that he didn't wear masks himself, but that he knew he wore masks is what Grant admired about him.

Gide continued. "Shakespeare is the one who immortalized the phrase: all that glitters is not gold."

"I'm afraid you've lost me," Grant said.

Gide stood up, and then he bent down to top off Grant's drink one more time. "I need to get back to my work." As he turned to go back in the house, he said, so softly that Grant was still wondering if he had heard right after the lawyer had gone inside, "You've already talked to him."

TWENTY-EIGHT

The phone next to Grant's bed rang at five in the morning. "Get dressed," Gerard said. "My men will bring you to Beauchamp's apartment. We have a warrant to search it."

In less than five minutes Grant was dressed and ready to go. The two bodyguards, different ones from the night before, were waiting for him. Grant was so eager to get to the apartment that one of the men had to pull him back when he tried to go through the door in the gate first.

As soon as he arrived at the apartment building, Grant was ushered up to the floor below the penthouse. The inspector was waiting for him.

"We have not gone in, yet," Gerard said. "We have called his regular phone, and we have tried to call up from this phone, the one next to his private elevator. We have gotten no response. We think he may have fled."

Grant knew very little about French law, but apparently Gerard had not been given the equivalent of a no-knock search warrant. "What now?"

Gerard held up a key. "To the elevator. We go up. But before we do, understand that the elevator opens up into an entrance that leads to the living room. The uniformed officers with the vests and shields will be in front. Several plainclothes officers will follow. We will be behind them."

Fair enough, Grant thought, since he was not armed.

Once the elevator was loaded, one of the men in front pushed a button and they slowly rose to the penthouse. The doors opened into an attractive entrance, a small room with a high ceiling, furnished with a hat stand with a tall mirror and two attractive chairs. Louis the XIV, Grant noted.

The four uniformed officers slowly advanced into the living room while the three plain-clothed officers backed them up from the doorway. Slowly the men worked their way into the apartment.

Gerard stepped from the elevator, and then he held up a hand to stop Grant. "One of my men will tell us when it is clear to enter."

Grant stepped to the doorway and admired the living room. It was both ornate and elegant, more like the room one might find in a palace instead of an apartment in Paris. At the same time, he thought it was cold. Every piece in the room was perfect for the décor and space, but none of it looked lived in. He also notice that the decorations were more along the lines of what a tourist would find in an expensive shop on the Champs-Élysées, but not the kind of art handled by Euro-Arts. Apparently Maurice was not a client of the company.

Gerard stood, silent, lost in his own thoughts. Grant wondered what he might be thinking. He was sure he would never know. To break the incredible silence of the apartment, Grant asked, "How were you able to get the search warrant?"

Gerard turned to stare at Grant, finally realizing the question had been directed at him. "Oh," he said, "we did have to wake some people, but your suggestions was a very good one. Some day I will have to ask what made you think of it. Beauchamp's dog, Rikki, was lodged during the exact dates of two dozen hits we believe were carried out by the Assassin. That was enough."

But not conclusive, Grant knew. Although Beauchamp had become careless of late, he was not quite sure if they had enough to hold him, and he doubted that the man was careless enough to leave anything incriminating behind. Depending on where he fled, they might not ever have a chance to arrest him.

One of the plainclothes detectives returned and said something quietly to Gerard. An eyebrow raised on the inspector's face. He nodded for Grant to follow and then led the way into the apartment.

Inspector Gerard was wrong. Maurice Beauchamp had not run. He was sitting in the atrium, waiting for them.

Gerard stopped in front of him, so Grant had to step around him to see. Beauchamp sat in a chair conveniently placed so he could look through an extensive collection of plants to the windows beyond. Although not a spectacular view, nor even a view of the rooftops of Paris that were interesting enough on their own, Beauchamp did have a view down a boulevard that led to the Champs-Élysées. The top of the Eiffel Tower could be seen in the distance over the buildings.

Maurice Beauchamp was looking in this direction, but he was not admiring the view. He was very dead. Rikki was stretched out at his master's feet. He had probably been asleep when Beauchamp reached down with the silenced gun and shot the dog in the back of the head. He probably did not mourn long. Instead it appeared he then put the barrel into his own mouth, pressing the silencer to the soft palate, and pulled the trigger. The gun was on the floor, near the dog. Beauchamp sat upright in his chair, his dead eyes staring through the plants to the windows beyond.

"It looks like Smith is going to have to find a new hobby," Grant said.

Gerard's lips twitched slightly, a hint of a smile. "My

man told me that the fireplace is filled with ashes. It appears that Monsieur Beauchamp burned papers before he took his life. He was apparently as good at burning papers as he was at killing people."

That's why the sadness, Grant realized. Gerard was afraid that only half the case would be solved. They had the hit man, but they did not have the client.

"He was paid top money because he was discreet," Grant said. "Apparently he remains discreet into death."

"I'm going to lead the search of the apartment. As unpleasant as it is, I ask that you remain here until the coroner arrives."

"Certainly," Grant said.

Gerard exited. Grant stood back to look at the man who had killed so many people so successfully for so long. He was not tall. He was a little chubby. His hair was thin on top. The only distinguishing characteristic at the moment about his face was the drool of blood that came from one corner of his mouth. He could have walked through a crowd and no one would have noticed him. In fact, if it hadn't been for the dog Rikki, Dubois might not have noticed him.

Grant wondered if Beauchamp recognized the irony in it. He had been done in by his dog.

But he wouldn't have known that, Grant thought, as he walked around the atrium, searching for ... what? A reason why the man had killed himself instead of running? From the looks of things, he lived very well. With his recent loss of business, perhaps he could no longer afford to live so well. He doubted that they would ever know. Beauchamp's life, as he knew it, was over. He killed himself. They were free to draw whatever conclusions they wanted to, he decided. Beauchamp was in no position to argue.

When he came back to the body from the other side, he

noticed the stand next to the chair. On it was a half-empty bottle of expensive wine and a crystal glass. Next to these was a cell phone.

Although he knew he shouldn't, Grant picked it up and flipped it open. The phone was on. He scrolled through the menus in the phone. The phone had been wiped clean. Beauchamp was thorough when it came to destroying evidence.

Almost. Under "Call History" was a phone number. It was the last call made by Beauchamp, and this was the one category he had overlooked when he erased everything else from the phone's memory. Grant took out a small notebook from his pocket and jotted down the number.

He could not resist. He punched in instructions for the phone to redial the number. A voice answered on the third ring, an angry one. The man said, "I told you never to call me again," and then he hung up. Grant recognized the voice.

He replaced the phone on the side table and waited for Gerard to return. The inspector arrived with the coroner. He directed the other man to the body, and then he led Grant from the room. In the living room he said, "Nothing. We of course will be looking to see if he has an office or another residence, but I doubt we will find anything. We will have to search to find his bank records, because he has even destroyed information about his accounts. Eventually we will find them, but I don't think we will find a safe, or a safe deposit box, or a friend holding things for him."

Friends? That was hard for Grant to imagine. "Do you know if he had friends?"

Gerard shrugged. "The apartment manager doesn't remember seeing him with anyone. He doesn't remember anyone going up to see him, at least no one who asked for directions."

Grant began to walk to the elevator. "I have some things to do," he said.

Gerard followed him and they stopped in front of the open doors. "Reports?" Gerard asked.

"I want to stop at the hospital and see Jill. Then I'm going back to the office to call James Smith, unless you want to do that. Then I need to get word to Sutherlin."

"I'll leave Smith to you. He will be disappointed that you found Beauchamp before him."

"We found him," Grant said.

Gerard nodded. "You could take all the credit," he said.

Grant laughed. "Not if we're going to work together again."

Grant stepped into the elevator and put his finger on the button to take him down. Before he pushed it, Gerard asked, "You wouldn't know who hired him to kill Tiffany Sutherby, would you?"

Grant smiled as he pushed the button and said as the doors began to close, "Yes, I do." The last sight he had was of the quizzical expression on the inspector's face.

TWENTY-NINE

As he walked into the hospital, he knew he still had too much to do, and he couldn't afford this time to see Jill. Gerard or one of his men would find the number in the phone eventually, and then someone would figure out that a call was made after Beauchamp was dead. Gerard would know that Grant made it, and he would begin piecing the parts together as Grant had done. Grant wasn't even sure he had the rest of the day before that happened.

Jill showed no signs of pleasure at seeing him. Next to her, in a chair pushed up close to the bed, was the image of the woman that Grant had seen in Jill after she had come out of surgery. Her mother had arrived. He introduced himself.

"I can only stay a few minutes," he said. "I came to tell Jill that the man who shot her is dead."

Jill, who had only briefly glanced at him when he walked in, now slowly turned her head to see his face. "Did you kill him?" she asked in a whisper.

He shook his head. "He killed himself."

She absorbed what he said, and then she finally asked, "Why?"

"After he made such a mess of the attack on you, I think he knew it was just a matter of time before we closed in on him. You can take some of the credit."

She nodded. "I guess I can."

He couldn't tell if that meant anything to her. It was just one more piece of information for her to take in and try to understand. Her senses were overwhelmed. He wasn't sure where she would be when she recovered. He was sure, though, that she wouldn't be quite the same. People who shot people, and people who got shot and survived never were.

He expressed pleasure at meeting her mother, and he excused himself to Jill. He had work to do.

Back at the office he called James Smith. Smith was absolutely silent as he explained that Beauchamp was dead and what had led up to it. When he was done, the only thing Smith could say was, "It all happened so quickly."

That was the way it was. If a crime was going to be solved, the solution often came suddenly with that one little piece of information. "It happens that way."

"Brilliant, you're in the country only two weeks and you've caught a man we couldn't catch for more than a decade of trying. Your bloody government will make a hero out of you."

"I don't plan to take all the credit. You, Gerard, and I worked together to get the man. We'll share in the glory." Grant could have easily given the other two men the credit, but he knew this was a break, and he could use it to leverage himself into a position he wanted, with the people he wanted. He had been a cop for a few years. He knew all about politics.

"Tell me everything again," Smith said.

Grant didn't want to waste the time, but he knew this was important to Smith. He went back over it again, recalling all the little details and passing them along.

When Grant finished, Smith said, "The dog ..." He could almost see him shaking his head at the other end of the line.

"I do have something for you to do," Grant said.

"Christ, anything."

He gave him the phone number from Beauchamp's cell phone. "I'm pretty sure it's a private line. I even know whose number it is. What I need to know is where the phone is located."

"If it's a private line, it will be a little tricky, but not much. I should have it for you in an hour. After I get that done, I'm going to find out everything I can about Maurice Beauchamp. I'll want it for me, and I'll also need it for our profilers."

"I'll be curious to hear what you find out," Grant said.

His next call was to Linda. She was in her room, packing, as she told him when he answered the phone. Walter wasn't doing well, and she needed to get back.

"Tell Walter the killer is dead," Grant said.

"You didn't …?" She left the question hanging.

She knew about the kid. She knew how hard it had been on him. She knew he had never recovered from it. "He killed himself, I think because he knew we were closing in on him."

"Oh good," she said, relieved. "You know you're too damned sensitive for the work you do. Come back and be a lawyer with me."

"Next vacation maybe I'll come visit," he said, knowing full well that he wouldn't have vacation time for almost a year, and that by then Linda would have moved on to another man.

"I'm going to hold you to your word. Is there anything I can tell Walter about the other?"

"The other?"

"The other part of the equation: The person who hired the killer."

"With any luck," Grant said, "I'll be seeing the man later today." He hung up without saying goodbye.

His final call was to Mark Trumbo. He would need to know what Grant had found out.

After Grant told Trumbo that Beauchamp was dead, the Legal Attaché said, "Okay, now I want you to start from the top and tell me how all of this worked again."

Grant did. In the end, he did a quick summary. "One of the services offered by Euro-Arts, discreetly, was to have reproductions of masterpieces painted by a group of talented, emerging artists. They liked the idea because they made some extra money. In reality these copies were never sold. They were just a front used by Euro-Arts to hide another aspect of their business: art theft. I knew that for sure when I got the list of Sutherlin's paintings. Each was a copy of a painting that had been stolen. They weren't copies; they were the originals and Sutherlin had paid Euro-Arts a fortune for them."

Trumbo interrupted. "But why would Sutherlin take the risk?"

"What risk? If anyone asked, he had documentation that these were re-creations."

"I still don't get it."

"That's because you don't have enough money. Rich people don't like to be told no. They don't like it when they can't have something they want. So they get it. Euro-Arts caters to spoiled, rich people."

"How many of these spoiled, rich people are we going to cause to clench their cheeks?" Trumbo asked, laughing at his own use of Grant's phrase.

"Quite a few, but most of them won't be Americans. Americans don't lust for art the way the Europeans and Japanese do."

"What happened with Sutherlin?"

"Since no one is talking, I can only guess. I think that Sutherlin, when he learned he was dying of cancer, decided to return the art to the world. What did he have to lose? He would be dead before he could be prosecuted. But to expose the truth about his paintings was to expose Euro-Arts. I'm pretty sure Beauchamp made a number of hits that Euro-Arts paid for. They had a contingency. They called it 'sending a message.' It was unlikely that they could get to Sutherlin to stop him, so they went after what they could reach: Tiffany Sutherby. She wasn't a saint, and she wasn't Sutherlin's favorite grandchild, but he got the message. Besides, he has other grandchildren he doesn't want to lose. They are, after all, his legacy."

"Why the other messages?"

"I suspect they were sent when clients didn't live up to an agreement."

"Will Sutherlin cooperate now?"

"Not until we have the person or persons from Euro-Arts locked safely away."

"And what chance do we have of that happening?"

"I'll let you know as soon as I find out," Grant said.

He received two phone calls within the next hour. Inspector Gerard called to say, "I appear to have made a mistake. Apparently permission was given to your government for you and Ms. St. Claire to carry guns before she was involved in the gun battle."

"Your government moves more quickly than mine," Grant said.

"After the fact, yes."

"Are you suggesting some kind of conspiracy?" Grant asked, knowing quite well that the inspector suspected more than that.

"You have been in this country for such a short time, and yet you already have powerful friends in high places."

"I hope that includes you, Inspector Gerard," Grant said, beginning to like the feel of diplomacy.

"You will go far," the inspector said, "especially with friends like me."

After the inspector hung up, Grant was relieved to realize that Gerard had not mentioned the phone number. He wanted this to be his little surprise.

The second call was from Smith. He had the address.

He only had to walk a few blocks. A few days before he had walked past the very shop and had noticed the paintings in the window. He never would have associated it with Euro-Arts, but now it all made sense. A small gallery in Paris, the Internet, a network of underworld connections, and secure cell phones or private phone lines: a perfect combination for attracting little attention.

He entered the shop and admired the small sculptures and the assortment of oil paintings on display. Each had a modest price tag, affordable for the well-healed tourist. Only a young woman was in the shop, a salesgirl.

"Bon jour," she said warmly.

"Hello, I'd like to see Kyle Hosteller about a painting."

"He's in his office on the third floor," she said, and then she pointed toward a staircase near the rear of the store.

"What's on the second floor?" he asked, more out of curiosity than anything else.

"We have a gallery of paintings by a collection of impressive young artists. Mr. Hosteller will be sure to show you," she said, and then she made eye contact and smiled brightly, just like she'd been trained to do, he imagined.

He returned the smile and headed for the stairs. Only one door was open at the top of the stairs, and Grant could see a man behind a desk in the room. A second door was marked W.C. A third was closed and had a lock on it. Storage, Grant thought.

He stood in the doorway and surveyed the man at work over a ledger book. He was over-weight and nearly bald.

He wore black-rimmed glasses with thick, thick lenses. He had the complexion of a man who ate too well and exercised too little. He did not look like a man who would hire someone to kill another person, but Grant knew he could and would. Kyle Hosteller pretended to be a minor character in a major enterprise, but he was not. He was the main player, and he was the enterprise. Both Gide and Sutherlin as much as told him so.

"Mr. Hosteller," Grant said.

The man was slow to respond. Grant was about to say his name again, when Hosteller finally looked up. "Yes?" he said.

Hosteller did not recognize the man he had ordered killed. Grant leaned in the doorframe and said, "The electronic age is a wonderful thing. A wealthy businessman in Japan calls you and says he would love to have a Rembrandt. He names the picture. You do a little research, and then you make a call. In a few days someone calls back and tells you that he can get the painting, and he names a price."

Hosteller was squinting at Grant through his thick lenses, his mouth slightly open as he listened to the narrative.

Grant continued. "One of your young, gifted artists paints a replica of the painting, while somewhere else in Germany, or England, or the United States, a painting is being stolen, usually from a private collection because it's easier, but sometimes from a museum. The latter really adds to the price.

"Should something go wrong, should someone fail to pay the price or deliver the goods, or should someone such as Walter Sutherlin decide to confess and return his artworks to society, you lift another phone and make a call. You probably have several people who can deliver a message for you, perhaps one who specializes in arson, or another who specializes in brutal beatings, or another—we called him the Assassin—who specializes in death."

Hosteller continued to stare with his mouth open, and he waited to see if Grant would go on. When it was clear that Grant was done, he said, simply, "Prove it. Prove any of it." He laughed and went back to his books.

"The Assassin is dead now, but he left behind some incriminating evidence."

"I don't know who you're talking about," Hosteller said without lifting his head.

"That was me who called you this morning. I was calling from the Assassin's apartment."

That got his attention. Again he was staring at Grant. "Who are you?" he asked.

"And once Sutherlin's artwork has been appraised and has been proven to be originals, the whole thing will start to unravel. You are very clever, but you are not clever enough. The police will have enough to begin an investigation, and, eventually they'll find something. It will seem like a small thing at first, but it will turn into your doom."

Hosteller's hand was moving from the desktop toward a drawer. He would have a gun there, Grant was sure. He could easily pull a gun himself and kill the man, claiming self-defense. But he didn't have a gun. He didn't want one.

"I want to know who you are," Hosteller said, his hand dropping out of sight.

Grant spun out of the doorway and took the steps down two at a time. Hosteller was too fat to catch up to him. On the second landing, he called back up the stairs, "I'm a man you tried to have killed. That proved to be a costly mistake for the Assassin, for you, and probably for a lot of clients of yours."

He could hear Hosteller moving toward the stairs, his gait ponderous and his footfall heavy. "You won't do well in prison," Grant said and then continued quickly down the stairs. He waved to the girl on the way out the door, and then he walked back to his office quite pleased with himself. As soon as he got back he would call Gerard and make sure Hosteller had no time to flee. And then he would stop by the bar on the corner and have a cold beer. He had earned it.

THIRTY

The rest of his week had a surreal quality to it for Grant. He received a phone call from Gerard the day after he had visited Hosteller, informing him that the man was now in custody and that he had hired, for a large retainer, Gilles Gide to defend him. Gerard also chided him about the cell phone number and the visit to Hosteller on his own. "I will expect better cooperation in the future," he warned.

The Assistant Secretary to the Assistant Secretary of State called to inform Grant that he would be receiving a citation signed by the Secretary of State. Both the ambassador and the Legal Attaché called to offer their congratulations.

By the end of the week, the story was breaking on both sides of the ocean, and Grant's name played a prominent part. He was now being referred to as an FBI associate, a State Department official, and a foreign representative to the President. Everyone was working overtime to have a little of his momentary glory rub off on them.

In the meantime he was too swamped to bask in the glory. Americans abroad still insisted on having their traveler's checks stolen, their passports lost, and their cars go missing. When he wasn't placating a fellow country-man, he was writing reports. The Legal Attaché's Office did send over a secretary to help him out, a pert and attractive American in her mid-twenties who made it clear she would do anything to help out Grant.

He settled for taking her to lunch each day. Sex in the workplace, he reminded himself, led to too many complications. That always brought him back to Jill, so he called her each day at the hospital. She became more responsive with each phone call. Learning that she could stay in Paris if she chose helped, although she wasn't sure if that was what she would do.

Linda called at the end of the week, shortly after Walter Sutherlin died. She told Grant that after Walter learned that Hosteller was in jail, he agreed to a signed deposition. He had indeed commissioned Hosteller to arrange for the artwork to be stolen. He provided Euro-Arts with his shopping list, and he asked no questions when the paintings arrived. Gide would have his work cut out for him, Grant thought, but he wouldn't bet yet that Hosteller would spend a lot of years in jail. He doubted that anyone would make a murder charge stick to him.

For the last three mornings Grant had awakened early and headed for the Cathédrale de Notre Dame. Each morning he had said his prayers, and each time he had lighted his candles, adding a new one for Beauchamp. Yesterday morning a priest, who introduced himself as le père Charles Perillat, had approached him and they had talked briefly. He had seen Grant's picture in the paper. That night the two had dinner together and shared a bottle of wine. The priest had asked him about the candles, and Grant, to his surprise, gave a lengthy explanation for each. Father Charles, the priest, had assured him that no guilt rested on Grant's shoulders.

Grant had not said anything at the time, because he did not believe that a man could give Grant a forgiveness that belonged to God, but when he walked back home that night he felt somehow relieved. Last night he had not dreamed about the boy.

James Smith called as well. He had learned a little about Beauchamp, but he was still doing research. Maurice had been an overweight, shy, and plain boy growing up. He was often picked on because he was also passive. His only two talents were playing minor characters in school productions and excelling at target pistol competitions. Smith did not know how he made the transition from that to a hit man.

Grant suggested, "Perhaps it was a teacher's advice. Don't teachers always tell us to follow our talents? He turned his talent for acting and shooting pistols into a successful career."

Smith did not see the humor in that. He was still depressed about the loss of his reason for being, but he did cheer up at the end of the conversation and tell Grant that he thought he had identified another hit man at work. Certainly he did not have the fame of the Assassin, but maybe this time they could catch this one more quickly.

By late in the afternoon Grant was ready for the weekend. He sent the secretary away early, much to her delight, and locked up the office. The sun was out and it was a warm day. Instead of going directly home, he decided to go to the Luxembourg Gardens. He would enjoy sitting in the sun near the pond and watch the children with their sailboats.

Gide had invited him to go out to dinner on Saturday night with the understanding that they would not talk about Hosteller. He would be glad to bring, if Grant did not mind, two other lawyers from his firm—women, both quite attractive. Grant accepted the offer, but without the women. He needed to find out where Jill fit in his life. Until then, he wouldn't be ready to see other women.

He found a chair near the pond and sat in the sun, feeling quite content. He had come here to put the past to rest and to start fresh. He now believed he could do both. On Sunday Jill was going back to her apartment. He promised to be there. He was feeling good enough about himself now that in time he thought he might be able to help Jill get over what she had been through.

The future had opened up to all sorts of possibilities. He turned his face to the sun to greet them all.